GRASSY KNOLL

BY

NANCY EVANS CONNORS

Inspired Forever Book Publishing
Dallas, Texas

Grassy Knoll

© 2018 Nancy Evans Connors

Inspired Forever Book Publishing™
"We Bring Inspiration to Life"
Dallas, Texas
(888) 403-2727

Printed in the United States of America

Library of Congress Control Number: 2018937002

Softcover ISBN-13: 978-0-9996258-4-2

CHAPTER ONE

"The people came to see me, not the Secret Service."
John Kennedy, Fort Worth, November 22, 1963

Fourteen-year-old Kate Gallagher was too excited to sleep. She stared into the darkness after repositioning herself and reversing her pillow for what seemed like the hundredth time. As pale gray light began to seep in around her window shade, she made out the dark shapes of her dresser and nightstand. She thought she could hear a light drizzle falling outside.

Kate took mental inventory of what she would need for the day ahead. She had chosen her clothes the night before, but she mentally ticked off the books and folders she'd need for school. Then her thoughts moved to the real focus of the day. She'd need her camera; good thing she had a new roll of film. She hoped the weather wasn't going to be too bad for picture taking.

Kate sighed with relief when she heard the soft thump of her mother's hairbrush being placed on the wooden surface of her dresser in the bedroom next door. Kate could always rely on her mother's ritual of getting up and running a brush through her hair before heading to the kitchen. For a light sleeper like Kate, this sound was her morning alarm clock. Not that she needed much of an alarm this morning.

Kate sprang out of bed and grabbed her bathrobe to stave off the early morning chill. She was so excited about the day ahead that her blood felt like it was carbonated as it raced through her body. This was the day! This was the day she was going to get to see President Kennedy and First Lady Jacqueline Bouvier Kennedy.

After a stop in the bathroom, Kate hurried down the hall to the kitchen. Her mother already had the light on and was in the pantry getting the coffee. "Hi, Mom."

"Gosh, Kate, you scared me. What are you doing up so early?" Her mother took the lid off the coffee can and began filling the percolator.

Kate moved toward the cabinet for the dishes and began to set the table for breakfast. "Oh, I've been awake for hours. I still don't see why I have to go to school today. I'm only going to be there about two hours anyway."

"Now don't start. We've been over this. If you want to try to see the president, then you'll go to school first.

2

It's nice of them to excuse you as it is. We'll go for the motorcade, and then you and Danny are both going back to school for the afternoon."

Kate sighed, but she knew it was futile to argue with her mother. It was just that she was so excited about actually seeing Kennedy. It was unbelievable enough that the country had actually elected the young president from Massachusetts, but to have him and the first lady come to Dallas was more than she'd ever dreamed. And because her dad had volunteered during the campaign, he had decided that all four of them would make the trip downtown.

The president's schedule had been printed in the newspaper yesterday. Her dad believed their best opportunity to see him wasn't at the airport but along the route his limousine would travel through the city on its way to the luncheon at the Trade Mart.

Kate's mother turned on the radio just as the tail end of the weather report mentioned morning showers clearing out by noon. The local news followed, and all of it focused on the biggest story of the day—the president's trip to Texas.

"In Fort Worth, the president and first lady will be joining several hundred Democrats for a 9:00 breakfast sponsored by the Chamber of Commerce. Following that event, the presidential party will travel four miles from the Hotel Texas to Carswell Air Force Base where they will board Air Force One for the short flight to Love Field. City officials

expect several thousand spectators to greet the president and first lady when they arrive in Dallas around 11:30 a.m.," continued the reporter.

"Kate, go tell your dad and brother that breakfast will be on the table in five minutes. And be sure Danny is wearing something decent."

Kate headed toward her parents' bedroom first. She could hear her dad humming as he shaved in the half bath adjoining the bedroom. "Dad, Mom said breakfast is almost ready."

"Okay, darling, I'll be right there." He stuck his head out of the open bathroom door just as she turned to leave. "Excited?" he asked with a twinkle in his eyes.

"Oh, Dad, I can hardly wait." Kate spoke dreamily. "Just think; I'm going to see JFK! It will be something to tell my grandkids about, won't it?"

Coming out of her reverie, Kate headed toward Danny's room. She knocked loudly on the door and called, "Danny, breakfast is almost ready; hurry up!"

Her eleven-year-old brother opened the door and came out into the hallway. "You don't have to yell. I'm coming," he replied, pulling a ratty old sweatshirt over his head.

"Danny, you can't wear that. You're going to see the president! Mom said to wear something decent. That faded old sweatshirt is a disgrace."

"Well, President Kennedy won't care what I wear; he won't even see me," Danny complained. Nonetheless, he returned to his room to change. Nothing irritated him more than having his older sister boss him around. But since the command came from his mother, it was simpler to comply than to argue.

Kate rushed into her own room and shut the door behind her. Fortunately, she had showered the night before and had her outfit ready to go. She quickly smoothed the sheets on her twin bed and pulled the blanket and comforter into place. She centered the pillow and tossed her favorite stuffed animals on top for the final touch. One rule you wouldn't think of breaking in this house was leaving the bed unmade. If she was honest about it, she, too, preferred the neat look of her room when the bed was made. She quickly donned her pleated skirt and sweater set, then added socks and penny loafers. A few strokes to her hair, a blast of hairspray, a touch of lipstick, and she was ready.

Kate opened her closet door and grabbed her camera off the shelf. She checked the back to make sure it was empty before opening it. She fumbled through her junk drawer and found the new package of film. Twelve shots. That should be enough to catch the motorcade as it passed by. She inserted the roll into the back of the camera and threaded the film into the sprockets. She snapped the case shut and gave the knob a few quick turns to make sure the film was ready for the first picture.

Kate returned to the kitchen, poured four glasses of orange juice, and set them on the table. Danny came in wearing the new sweater his mother had bought him last week and received a smile of approval in response. When Frank Gallagher walked in, the family sat down to its usual weekday breakfast of bacon and eggs.

Glancing at the light rain peppering the window, Mr. Gallagher commented, "Looks kind of nasty out there."

"Yes, but the weather forecast is for clearing skies and mild temperatures," replied Mrs. Gallagher.

"How close will we be to President Kennedy, Dad?" Danny asked. "Will it be crowded, or will we be able to see him up close?"

"I don't know the answer to that, son. It just depends on the crowds. I think most people will go to Love Field to see him, but I can't be sure. I looked at the map in the paper and picked out a place to wait near Houston and Elm. There's an embankment there where the limousine will turn to get on the freeway. The motorcade is supposed to pass there sometime after noon," Mr. Gallagher added, "so your mother will pick you kids up at school at 11:00. She's bringing you to my office where we'll park the car and take a bus to the barricades. There's no sense in trying to park any closer than that."

They turned their attention once again to the radio station.

"I am reporting live from the parking lot of the Hotel Texas in downtown Fort Worth where a crowd of several hundred workers are braving the rain and chill as they wait for President Kennedy to appear. This crowd of blue collar workers has been told that Mr. Kennedy will personally make an appearance to thank them for their ongoing support."

"I don't get it. Why is JFK going out to the parking lot, Dad?" Danny stopped eating as he awaited his father's explanation.

"These are the people who helped put Kennedy in office, but they don't have big money. They can't afford to take time off work and pay a lot of money to attend the breakfast in his honor, so he's going outside to talk to them first. Pretty savvy of him, really. You can't help but be impressed with someone who will go outside in this weather and shake hands with regular everyday people."

The family continued to talk about the day ahead while they finished eating and listened to the radio. According to the news report, the president would lunch in Dallas and then travel to Austin for the evening. Then he and the first lady would enjoy a well-deserved rest at the vice-president's ranch where a large barbecue would be held for the people of Johnson City to meet them. Even more special, this was First Lady Jackie Kennedy's first trip with her husband since the loss of their premature infant son in August.

Mrs. Gallagher stood up with her coffee cup in hand and started clearing the table. "Okay, kids, finish up and go brush your teeth. We'll be ready to leave shortly."

Danny and Kate both carried their breakfast dishes to the sink and hurried to their rooms to finish their morning routines. Their dad always dropped them off at school on his way to work, but this morning their mother was driving all of them so she could keep the car and come pick them up later for the trip downtown. There was nothing routine about this day, November 22, 1963.

CHAPTER TWO

"Mrs. Kennedy is organizing herself. It takes longer, but, of course, she looks better than we do when she does it."

John Kennedy, Fort Worth, November 22, 1963

Barbara Gallagher pulled up in front of the elementary school where Danny was in the sixth grade. Danny opened the door and hopped out with a casual "See you later" thrown over his shoulder. Driving a few blocks further, Mrs. Gallagher pulled up in front of Kate's junior high school.

Kate scooped up her math and English textbooks as well as her three-ring binder and some folders. "Mom, I'm leaving my camera here in the backseat, okay?"

"That's fine. Just be sure you're waiting out front on time. Have a good morning."

Kate pulled up the hood on her raincoat and leaned into the front seat to give each of her parents a swift kiss on the cheek before stepping out into the rain and mist. She hurried up the steps and into the front doors. On mornings like this, students were allowed to go either to the cafeteria or to the auditorium until the bell rang. She made her way to the auditorium where she knew her friends would be sitting in the back row, the usual meeting place unofficially reserved for eighth graders.

"Hey, Kate!" Judy called out. "Do you have your math homework done?"

"Yes, but I'm not giving it to you," Kate smiled at her best friend. "Do you need help?" Kate slipped into an empty seat between Judy and another classmate, Gail.

Gail and the girls to her right were busy discussing the social event of the weekend, a slumber party being thrown by Brenda Gleason, another classmate. Registering that, Kate turned back to Judy.

"Yeah, I couldn't figure out those last five problems," Judy explained as she pulled her homework out of her binder. Kate studied the paper Judy thrust in front of her and began explaining the steps to solving the equations. Out of one ear, she heard Gail beginning to argue with the boys in front of her.

"Well, he shouldn't even be in Dallas. No one wants him here. You know he wouldn't even be president if his dad hadn't bought the election," Gail declared.

Johnny Underwood nodded his head vigorously in agreement. "Yeah, my dad says the Kennedys are taking over the country. I can't believe he appointed his own brother attorney general."

"Kennedy just wants to become friends with *Cube-ER*," quipped Tim Bertini, the class clown. Everyone laughed at Tim's attempt to mimic the president's New England accent as he continued playing to the crowd. "Here in *Ah-MUHR-ica*, we don't like the Kennedys."

Kate began to feel uncomfortable with the way her friends were attacking the president. She knew they were merely parroting the attitudes of their parents, but she wished they would think for themselves sometimes. "Come on, you guys," she spoke up. "Whether you like it or not, JFK is our president, and you should show a little respect."

Kate had always been at odds with her friends on the subject of politics. While her own Catholic family had supported Kennedy's race for the presidency, most of her friends' families had opposed him and everything he stood for. Even though Texas was a stronghold for the Democratic Party, voters in Dallas leaned toward the conservative brand of politics represented by Governor John Connally, not the liberal version represented by a northern president. The fact that John Kennedy was the first Catholic to ever be elected president was another thing that bothered many people.

"I'd love to see Jackie Kennedy," interjected Judy, turning away from her math to join the conversation. "I wish they'd let us out of school today to go to the airport."

"I'm going," Kate said quietly.

"What?" shrieked Judy. "You're going to Love Field?"

"No, we're going to stand along the motorcade somewhere downtown. My mom's picking me up at 11:00," Kate explained. "My dad planned for our whole family to go. He says this is a moment in history."

"Oh, my gosh!" shrilled Judy. "Be sure to tell me everything about Jackie. I want to know what she wears, how she looks, everything. Maybe you'll get to meet her!"

It was strange how in spite of the wide dislike for the president, everyone seemed to love the stylish first lady. Women and girls alike couldn't help but study every picture showing the beautiful clothes and hats worn by the elegant Mrs. Kennedy.

Kate laughed. "I doubt I'll meet her. I'm not even sure how well I'll be able to see, but I'll share what I can. I'm hoping to get some pictures, and I'll try to get one of the first lady for you."

Gail snorted and flipped her long hair over her shoulder. "Well, don't bore *me* with it. I couldn't care less about those rich snobs."

Just then the first bell rang, and everyone stood to gather their belongings and head toward their lockers.

●◆◆◆◆◆◆◆◆◆●

Third period, Kate had social studies. Mr. Barrett was her favorite teacher, always making the class lively and interesting, and today was no exception. Right after the bell rang, he held up the morning's edition of the *Dallas News.*

"How many of you saw this morning's headlines?" He scanned the class for a show of hands and then read aloud, "President's Visit Seen Widening State Democratic Split."

He then read another headline: "Storm of Political Controversy Swirls around Kennedy on Visit."

He thrust the paper aside and continued to probe the class. "Who can tell me what controversy the paper is talking about?"

The class was off and running. For the next half hour, Mr. Barrett led a lively discussion about the president's visit to Texas. When students made outlandish comments about the president, Mr. Barrett deftly moved them toward facts rather than emotion. He reviewed the structure of Texas politics with its conservative and liberal Democrats at war with each other. He explained how Governor John Connally and Vice

President Lyndon B. Johnson represented the conservative wing of the party while JFK appealed to the more liberal wing of the party.

"There's another interesting story in today's paper," the teacher said. "Anyone leaf back to section four?" He demonstrated this and looked up to comment. "It seems that former Vice President Richard M. Nixon is also in Dallas today. Why is that ironic?"

"Because Nixon lost to Kennedy," someone called out.

"That's right, class. Let's not forget that John Kennedy is a minority president who narrowly defeated Nixon in 1960 in the Electoral College. How is that possible? How can a candidate get the most votes and at the same time lose the election?"

The discussion continued, crescendoing to loud arguments at times. Finally it was time for Kate to hand her note to Mr. Barrett and ask to be excused before the bell since her mother was picking her up shortly.

"Kate, this note says that you and your family are going downtown for the motorcade. That's great. We'll expect a full report on Monday, won't we class?" he commented as he initialed the note.

Kate nodded, picked up her books, and left the room. After stowing her books in her locker and checking out in the front office, she hurried out front to where her mother waited.

"You're right on time," Mrs. Gallagher commented.

"Yes, I thought 11:00 would never get here!" Kate exclaimed.

"Would you go in and get your brother?" Mrs. Gallagher asked as she pulled up in front of Danny's school.

"Sure, Mom."

Danny was already in the school office, waiting on a bench. His face lit up when he saw his sister coming through the door. He quickly stood and followed her. "Boy, you wouldn't believe the razzing from my friends about going to this motorcade. Do you think Mom and Dad are the only ones in Dallas who voted for Kennedy?"

Kate laughed. "I doubt it, but it does seem that way sometimes, doesn't it."

She smiled at the office clerk who took the signed note, confirmed that Danny would return after lunch, and checked him out.

Kate and Danny left the office, hurrying out the front door. Laughing at their sudden freedom from the confines of school, they raced each other to the car, each seeking the coveted front seat.

CHAPTER THREE

"I am happy to be in your city today."
John Kennedy, Love Field, November 22, 1963

"**W**hy does she always get to sit in front?" griped Danny as he flung himself into the back seat.

"Because I'm the oldest, Squirt," replied Kate in a satisfied tone. "Hand me my camera before you sit on it."

Taking the Kodak her brother thrust into her hand, Kate began looking through the viewer and double checking to make sure it was wound and ready to go. "You think I'll be able to get any pictures, Mom?"

"I don't know, Kate. You can sure try." Her mother leaned forward to make sure it was safe to make a left turn through the intersection. "At least the rain has pretty well stopped. Now if the sun would just come out."

Barbara Gallagher snapped on the car radio. "...
*aboard Air Force Two with Vice President Johnson and
Mrs. Johnson. Both Air Force One and Two are expected to
land shortly at Love Field, where a throng of several thousand people await to greet the thirty-fifth president of the
United States making this landmark trip to Dallas."*

"Mom, why is the president flying to Dallas when
it's so close to Fort Worth?" asked Danny.

"I'm not sure. I guess they thought they'd have better security if they fly rather than drive the thirty-three
miles. It does seem silly to take such a short flight,
but maybe it has something to do with the president's
schedule. They can definitely beat the traffic by flying."

"But they could have used helicopters," argued
Danny.

"True, but they'd need quite a few. There are lots
of people traveling with the president and vice president. I think you'll be surprised when you see how big
the motorcade is."

"Just think. The president had breakfast in Fort
Worth, then he'll have lunch in Dallas, and dinner
tonight in Austin. Wow," commented Kate. She turned
to face her mother. "Some of the kids said awful things
about the Kennedys. And, of course, Tim was showing
off and mimicking the president's accent again."

"What did he do?" Danny wanted to know.

"He imitated the way the president pronounces 'Cuba' and words like that. I'll bet the people in the Northeast think we sound just as funny here in Texas."

"Boy, that's for sure. When your dad and I first met, he used to tease me about my Texas drawl." Barbara Gallagher smiled as she remembered the occasion on which she'd met her Midwesterner husband.

"Mr. Barrett wants me to report to the class on Monday," Kate shared. "I'm the only one actually going to see the motorcade."

"Yeah, my teacher wants me to do a report, too," added Danny.

"Mom, why do so many people resent President Kennedy?" asked Kate.

"I'm not sure they actually resent him," her mom replied. "Here in Dallas, he's not that popular, but you have to remember that he did win the election. Now, if people would just give him a chance and let him do his job."

Twenty-five minutes later, the car was parked in Frank Gallagher's reserved slot behind the building where he worked. Danny had gone in to get his dad, and now the family of four was ready to go.

"Mom, I'm hungry," Danny suddenly announced.

"You're always hungry! I made some sandwiches, but I thought you could eat them on the way back to school."

"*Pleeeease?*" begged Danny with a hangdog look.

"Oh, all right. I made you an extra one anyway." Barbara Gallagher opened the trunk and dug through a paper bag to give Danny a peanut butter and jelly sandwich. "There's lemonade in the thermos jug. Anyone ready for a cup?"

Danny nodded and his mother filled a paper cup and handed it to him. She shook her head when she saw that her son had already wolfed down three-fourths of his sandwich.

Looking at his watch, Mr. Gallagher said, "We're running a bit ahead of schedule. Since it's stopped raining, let's forget the bus and walk."

Danny jammed the last bite of his sandwich in his mouth, gulped down the lemonade, and tossed the cup in the trunk. The day was getting nicer, so Kate and her mother left their raincoats and umbrellas behind with the cup. Mr. Gallagher retrieved a small gray plastic transistor radio and then slammed the trunk shut.

Kate looked up at the billowing gray clouds that had wallpapered the sky all morning. A few patches of blue were just beginning to peek through the mist. She and Danny took off at a brisk pace up the sidewalk as their parents followed. Traffic seemed heavier than usual as they got closer to the parade route. Scores of people were streaming out of office buildings and filling up the sidewalk. Several people were clutching cameras or transistor radios while others chatted excitedly, but a few carried unfriendly protest signs with words such as "Yankee, Go Home!" and "You're a Traitor."

"Let's stay away from Main Street," suggested Mr. Gallagher. "There's bound to be lots of people there since that's the way the motorcade is coming."

They cut over to the next block and then turned south. By the time they'd walked several more blocks, the sun was occasionally nosing its way through the clouds. As only happens in Dallas in November, the chilly fog and rain of the early morning were giving way to heat and humidity. Kate was beginning to regret wearing her cardigan, but it was too late now.

As they approached Houston Street, Kate spied large wooden barricades at the intersection. A traffic policeman stood amongst them frantically signaling the stream of cars urgently trying to get to their destinations.

As they waited for a signal to cross the street, Mr. Gallagher looked around. "This is Dealey Plaza," he announced. "See that grassy embankment over there?"

he pointed to a grassy hill with surprisingly few people on it. "That's where I think we'll have the best vantage point."

CHAPTER FOUR

"We're in nut country now."

John Kennedy, Dallas, November 22, 1963

A t the corner of Houston and Elm, the Gallaghers stood waiting for the traffic cop to signal their turn to cross the busy street. The open square before them was a funnel for downtown Dallas as Main, Elm, and Commerce Streets all met there.

Traffic continued to crawl as ever more people intent on seeing the motorcade lined the sidewalk and jockeyed for position. Kate watched the policeman's arms gyrate as he orchestrated the heavy flow of traffic.

Mr. Gallagher pointed across to a large triangular grassy slope. "That's where we're headed. The motorcade is supposed to turn here and go right by there."

A whistle blew, and the crowd hurried into the street. Kate looked to her right at a red brick building. The sign on the front read Texas School Book Depository. Glancing up, she counted seven floors. Several windows facing the street were open, and she could see people leaning out, laughing and pointing as they ate their sandwiches and drank soft drinks.

"Boy, the people who work there will have a great view," commented Danny, and Kate nodded in agreement.

Compared to the crowds on Main Street, the numbers were sparse at Dealey Plaza. Frank Gallagher led his family along the sidewalk bordering Elm Street until he veered right and started walking up a set of steps dissecting the grassy triangle. Straight ahead was an ornate white memorial pavilion that curved behind a shallow pool and fountain. The top of the steps offered a good lookout over the intersection. Surprisingly, not too many people had chosen this vantage point to watch the procession.

"Dad, how come there aren't any television cameras here?"

"Well, Danny, I think most of them are at Love Field. Then they're going to televise the president's luncheon talk at the Trade Mart. It's easier to film indoors," Mr. Gallagher explained. "They're expecting 2,500 Dallas big shots at the luncheon."

Kate heard the wailing of a siren and pivoted to her left. Was the motorcade coming?

CHAPTER FOUR

Instead she saw an ambulance pull to a stop on Houston Street where a motorcycle policeman and several bystanders were huddled around a figure on the ground. In a hurried motion, the person was lifted onto a stretcher and positioned in the back of the open ambulance. Within a couple of minutes, the emergency vehicle sped past Kate. She saw it head downhill toward the triple underpass and realized it was probably going to nearby Parkland Memorial Hospital. "I wonder what happened," she said to her dad.

"I don't know, honey. Could be someone fainted or even had a heart attack."

Kate turned back to the scene surrounding her. She noticed that cars were still being allowed to pass on Houston Street, so the motorcade must not be close yet. She scanned the crowd and noticed many people holding transistor radios pressed to their ears. "Dad, turn on your radio and see what's going on."

Mr. Gallagher took his radio from his jacket pocket, turned the dial, inserted the small earpiece into his right ear, and stared intently as he listened. "Announcer says the motorcade is running about five minutes behind. Evidently the president asked them to stop so he could shake hands with people in the crowd."

Kate sighed with impatience. She continued inspecting the crowd and decided to snap a few background pictures. She took one picture looking across

25

at the crowd along Houston Street. Another picture included the crowd in front of the bronze statue of Mr. Joseph Dealey, founder of the *Dallas News*, for whom the plaza was named. For her third shot, she turned left and photographed the front of the Texas School Book Depository. She noticed the Hertz clock on the roof of the depository; the time was 12:24.

She turned in a circle and looked behind her to a railroad trestle. Uninteresting. She then turned right and looked over the rest of the nearby crowd. Her dad had really chosen a great location for viewing the procession. Few people shared this grassy area; most onlookers had chosen the opposite side of the street. Several held cameras, and two women even had the new Polaroid camera. They were laughing and talking while they experimented with their cameras. An elderly man behind them focusing an 8-millimeter movie camera on the crowd caught Kate's eye. How she wished she had one of those!

"Kate, look up there!" Grabbing her right arm, Danny interrupted her reverie.

"What?"

"Look at that Secret Service man sitting up there in the window!" Danny pointed.

Kate gazed up at the Book Depository and caught a quick glimpse of the silhouette of a man holding a rifle before he backed away from an open window on the sixth floor of the building. "That looks like a good lookout position," she said.

"You think he'd really shoot anybody who tried to hurt the president?"

"I suppose that's his job, to protect the president."

"Boy, I'd like to be a Secret Service agent. Wonder how many there are?" Danny looked around at the bystanders to see if he could detect any other agents. He focused on clean-cut men in suits wearing sunglasses, looking for any telltale walkie-talkies. That was usually a sign they were agents listening to directions from their commander.

"I imagine the motorcade itself will be surrounded by Secret Service men, Danny. Jackie Kennedy has agents assigned to her, too. Just think. If our dad were president, we'd be followed everywhere by our own bodyguards. I don't think I'd like that; would you?"

Kate's conversation with Danny was cut short by the shrill warning whistle given by the traffic policeman. Dark uniformed policemen began frantically pushing the crowds behind barricades and motioning traffic off the streets.

At last, the motorcade was coming.

CHAPTER FIVE

*"Mr. Kennedy, you can't say that Dallas isn't friendly
to you today."*

Mrs. John Connally, November 22, 1963

Danny practically jumped up and down with excitement while Kate felt a tingling of anticipation and craned her neck in an attempt to catch first sight of the motorcade. According to the radio, the procession was more than twenty vehicles in length and spread over half a mile. Still out of sight, the lead car had turned the corner from Main Street onto Houston, according to the radio announcer.

"I think I see them!" Kate proclaimed a moment later. She brought her camera up and began to peer through the viewer, waiting for the first clear shot of the motorcade. A single police car led the way followed a half block later by the heart of the procession.

First came a standard white sedan. Behind it was the midnight blue 1961 Lincoln presidential limousine brought in especially from Washington. It was flanked by four motorcycles. They were still too far away for a good picture, but Kate could see that the convertible was open.

"They're riding with the top down," she called out excitedly.

Kate quickly snapped her first picture of the historical event as the line of cars approached. She focused on the president's car. Texas Governor John Connally and his wife Nellie sat on jump seats in front of the president and first lady. Kate's view of President Kennedy was temporarily blocked by the large ten-gallon hat worn by the governor, so she moved her attention down the line of vehicles. She didn't recognize anyone in the second car, but the third convertible held the vice president and Mrs. Johnson along with Senator Yarborough.

As the pilot car neared Elm, it made a slow left turn toward them. Once it passed, Kate had a clear view of the presidential limousine as it neared the intersection. She could see the bright pink of the first lady's suit and her small pillbox hat. Both the president and Mrs. Kennedy beamed at the crowd. The president's famous smile seemed genuine and appreciative of those who had come out to greet him. The first lady held a large bouquet of deep red roses while the president lifted his hand in a wave. People in the crowd called out and cheered.

"Let's move closer, Danny." Kate grabbed her brother's arm and pulled him along. They quickly moved downhill by a Stemmons Freeway sign near the curb where Kate hoped to get several close-ups. The limousine had now made the left turn onto Elm, and Kate quickly snapped a picture and advanced the film to be ready for the next one.

The Lincoln was no more than fifty yards away now and creeping along at a very slow speed. Kate had a clear view of the lovely first lady's face. She had promised Judy a picture, so she took a snapshot and advanced the film quickly. She was just about to take another photo when the sudden popping of a fire-cracker got her attention.

"What was that?" Danny asked, a puzzled expression on his face. Kate jerked her head around in confusion and quickly turned back to face the limousine.

The president had his hand to his cheek and seemed to brush something from it as the car continued to move forward slowly. Now the Lincoln was less than 20 feet from where they stood. Kate snapped her next picture without consciously taking aim.

This time the sound was more distinct as the sharp crack of gunfire echoed through the plaza. Governor Connally turned quickly and began to fall over in slow motion. Kate inhaled sharply as her eyes darted to the president, who grasped his own bloody throat and began collapsing toward the roses now scattered in the seat.

Bystanders became aware of the danger. Some started screaming while others whimpered. A few onlookers turned to look up the grassy embankment toward a picket fence. Others whipped their heads back and forth, trying to take in the scene. Someone yelled, "Get down!"

Kate stood frozen as people around her began hitting the ground. Time stood still. Somewhere in the far recesses of her mind, she heard the sound of her mother's voice calling out to her and Danny. When Danny jerked her hand in an attempt to pull her down, Kate dropped her camera. She squatted on her haunches, never taking her eyes off the road before her.

A third shot rang out just as the president's limousine passed by.

Kate watched in horror as the back right side of the president's head exploded into red mist.

After a couple of seconds, the Lincoln seemed to buck and then pick up speed.

The sound of panicked screaming found its way into Kate's mind. People were running across the grass or lying on the ground with their hands cupping their heads. Her eyes still riveted to the presidential car, she struggled to comprehend the tragedy she had just witnessed.

The Lincoln had now passed her, but Kate had a clear view of the rear of the vehicle. She saw the first lady begin to crawl out of her seat and onto the back of the Lincoln. She watched a Secret Service agent from the second vehicle jump out, run up to the presidential limousine, and leap onto the back bumper. She watched him lean forward and push Jackie Kennedy back into her seat just as the vehicle accelerated and entered the darkness of the underpass.

The scene lasted mere seconds, but it was long enough for Kate to register the dark red saturating the front of the first lady's suit.

One by one, two dozen vehicles accelerated, closed ranks, and roared after the limousine. In less than a minute, the final car had disappeared from Dealey Plaza. Only the echo of a myriad of sirens filled the air as police vehicles chased the motorcade onto Stemmons Freeway.

CHAPTER SIX

"Any man who is willing to exchange his life for mine can do so."

John Kennedy, October 1963

For a few moments, Dealey Plaza was quiet. After all the running, all the screaming, and all the screeching of tires, there was absolutely no sound at all. People sat on the grass staring at the empty street. As the reality of what they had witnessed sank in, sobbing began to penetrate the air.

"Kate?"

The sound of her brother's voice shook Kate from her daze. Slowly, she stood up and looked around. She noticed her camera on the ground and wondered how it had gotten there. Woodenly, she stooped and picked it up.

"Kate?" Danny's voice held a tremor as he stared into his sister's eyes. "Is he dead?"

At first, Kate couldn't find her voice. She licked her lips and framed her words carefully. "I don't know, Danny." Then she looked into his probing eyes and knew he'd seen what she had. She took a deep breath and whispered, "Yes, I think so."

Kate turned to where she'd last seen her parents and saw them both still on the ground. She hurried toward them with Danny close on her heels.

Their mother was lying on the ground, her hose torn and her knees muddy, sobbing hysterically as their father held her and spoke soothing words in her ear.

He glanced up at his children. "Are you kids all right?"

The pain Kate saw reflected in his eyes was almost her undoing, but she nodded.

Danny squatted by his mother. Shaken by her tears, he was at a loss for something to do or say. "Mom, it's going to be okay."

"No, Danny. It's not okay; it will never be okay again." His mother cried harder as his dad patted her back and said nothing.

Kate trembled. She felt light-headed. She turned away from the wrenching scene and looked about her. What a different sight this was from a few minutes earlier. Many people had already disappeared from the streets and embankment, but others seemed unable to move. The old man with the movie camera was carefully examining his camera and speaking to the lady beside him. A few people were getting off the ground and pointing up toward the railroad trestle while others gestured toward the fence behind the pavilion. One woman screamed and took off running.

Shouts from the intersection drew Kate's attention. Several uniformed policemen began running in all directions. One pointed to the Book Depository and headed toward the door while others fanned out in different directions. Sirens pierced the air as squad cars rounded the corner from Main onto Houston Street.

"Do you think it's safe to stay here?" Barbara Gallagher asked her husband as she gulped for air and tried to calm herself. She wiped her face and got to her feet, brushing absently at the grass and dirt on her dress. The shock of the moment was subsiding, and now her concern was for her family. "What if there's a madman on the loose?"

"I don't know," her husband answered as he contemplated the question. He looked around and helped steady his wife, then pulled her close.

"Everyone stay put," called an officer from the street. "No one leave until we get statements."

Kate looked beyond the officer and saw a motor-cycle policeman in the middle of Elm Street. The windshield of his motorcycle was splattered with red gore. The policeman removed his stained helmet and began to rub furiously at the blood. A few feet away, another bystander was bent over, retching into the grass. Sickened by the realization that these men had been next to the limousine when the shots had been fired, Kate felt the bile rise in her own throat.

"Dad, where's your radio? Turn it on and see if we can find out what's happening," Danny asked.

"Do you think it's possible he's alive?" asked Barbara Gallagher with a note of optimism in her voice. Kate and Danny looked at each other without answering. They'd been closer to the scene than their mother. They didn't want to dash her hopes, so neither said anything.

Frank Gallagher picked his transistor radio up off the ground and removed the earpiece. He turned the volume up for all of them to hear. All they heard was music. Mr. Gallagher began moving the dial in hopes of finding a news report. "Maybe the stations don't know yet," he said. He glanced up at the Hertz clock and saw that fewer than five minutes had passed since the shots rang out.

For the next few minutes, the Gallaghers remained quiet and watched the frenzy of activity taking place around them. More and more patrol cars arrived in the plaza. Other officers wearing the uniform of the sheriff's department also appeared on the scene since their headquarters were just half a block away at the county building.

In a few minutes, several deputies rushed over to the grassy embankment. Kate saw one couple talking to a deputy and pointing up the incline toward the parking lot behind the picket fence. The officer withdrew his gun from its holster and took off running in that direction.

"This can't be happening," said Barbara Gallagher. "We're a modern country; things like this just happen in history books."

"Hold on. I think I've got something," interrupted Frank Gallagher. He turned the volume up louder on his small radio.

" ... *report that three shots rang out as the president's motorcade passed through downtown Dallas. Stay tuned for more details on this breaking story.*"

"That's it, I guess. Nothing on his condition," reported Mr. Gallagher.

"Dad, I saw a man with a rifle," said Danny in a small voice.

"You what?" asked Mr. Gallagher in an incredulous tone.

"I saw a man up there." Danny pointed up to the sixth floor of the Book Depository.

"I saw him too, Dad. Well, just a quick glance," added Kate.

"Why didn't you say something?" their dad asked in amazement.

"We thought it was the Secret Service," Danny replied.

"Frank, I don't think the shots came from there," Barbara Gallagher stated. "I could swear I heard shots from that direction." She pointed up the incline to the right toward the picket fence.

While her parents debated the direction of the gunfire, Kate and Danny began their own dialogue.

"You don't think he was the killer do you, Kate, that man in the window?"

"I don't know, Danny. It all happened so fast. At first I thought it was just a firecracker. Then it was all just a blur." Kate's voice trailed off as she rewound the videotape in her mind to examine the details recorded there. She really wasn't sure where the shots had come from. She had been so intent on watching the president and first lady that she hadn't registered the origin of the shots. Besides, there was an echo effect in the canyon-like plaza since brick and stone buildings surrounded it.

Over the next few minutes, sightseers began to gather at Dealey Plaza. Eyewitnesses turned to those around them and shared what they'd seen and heard. Policemen moved among the bystanders interrogating those who had witnessed the shooting. Fire trucks arrived and barricaded Elm Street.

Kate's legs had grown weak, so she sank onto the grass, and Danny plopped down beside her. An invisible yet unbreakable bond had developed between the two siblings.

A police officer soon approached the Gallaghers. He started questioning Kate's parents in a brisk professional manner, asking how long they'd been standing there and if they'd seen the shooting.

Barbara Gallagher started crying again. Her voice cracked as she tried to respond. "I, we ... " She could not continue.

Frank Gallagher stepped closer and put a comforting arm around her. "Yes, Officer, my wife and I both saw it. Or, we heard it."

As her parents began to share their impressions, Kate glanced at Danny. They would be next. She listened to her parents' versions and realized they had not actually seen the impact of the third shot since they had dropped to the ground.

"And what about you, Miss? Did you see anything?"

Kate nervously stood back up. In spite of the fact that she was starting to feel chilled and shaky, she knew she had to tell what she'd seen. She glanced at Danny and began to describe exactly what she'd witnessed.

The officer nodded and wrote short notes on a small pad as she narrated her story.

Kate spoke softly. She didn't want her mother to hear what the last bullet had done to the president's head, but she could tell from her father's face that he heard it all and was stunned by her close-up account.

"Where were you standing?"

Kate pointed down the incline to the curb.

"And where did the shots come from?"

Kate scanned the scene; she wasn't sure what to say. She glanced over the officer's shoulder and saw her dad nod. She told about seeing the man in the window of the Book Depository holding a rifle. She also told the officer she wasn't positive if that's where the shots had come from.

"Maybe there were two shooters," offered Danny. Now he had the officer's attention and went on to give his account of the events.

Although Danny's description of the shooting was very similar to Kate's, he had seen the person in the window much longer and more clearly than she had.

"He sat up there in the window like a statue, and he had a long rifle sloped across his chest." Danny's voice wobbled when he came to the part where he described seeing the third shot tear the president's head apart.

Kate stepped closer to Danny so he could feel her arm pressed up against him. She felt him lean into her for comfort.

"Okay, we're going to need sworn affidavits from all of you," the policeman stated. "Don't go anywhere."

Nudging her brother a few yards from their parents, Kate spoke softly to him.

"It's not your fault, Danny. You've got to believe that. Nothing you could have said could have stopped it; there wasn't time."

Her brother didn't say a word. He just stared at his feet, then turned and walked a few feet away.

Kate didn't follow him. She knew he needed time to himself.

A few minutes later, another officer came to interview them. Once more they each told their stories, and once more the words were carefully recorded into a notepad.

Somehow, talking about it made it even more real. It was gradually starting to sink in that they were eyewitnesses to an event that would change life, and change them, forever.

Kate noticed that Danny was now trembling as much as she was. The initial shock was giving way to a full realization of what they had observed. The president had been shot, possibly murdered, right before their eyes.

"They're coming on the air with an update," said Mr. Gallagher.

" ... *President is said to be in critical condition. He was rushed to Parkland Memorial Hospital in Dallas, Texas, where emergency teams are fighting to save his life. Two priests were seen hurrying into the emergency room.*"

"That means he's alive," said Kate's mother, hope surging through her words.

"Maybe," said her father. "But they could just be waiting to give him Last Rites." He glanced at the kids when he said this, and they knew he was trying to prepare their mother for the worst.

"Okay, folks, we want all of you to move across the street to the county building, to Sheriff Decker's office where you will give your statements."

Kate turned around at the sound of the loud instructions to see a deputy motioning everyone on the embankment to move across Houston Street. Along with everyone else, she made her way down the incline to the sidewalk. Policemen were careful to confine the witnesses to the sidewalk as they kept Elm Street cordoned off.

They continued north past the Book Depository until they crossed the intersection at Houston and Elm.

As they turned right, Kate stopped. Turning, she slowly took in the scene one more time. She lifted her eyes to the sixth floor of the Book Depository and then looked back down the block at where she and Danny had stood at the curb. She raised her camera for one final shot even though she knew it wasn't really necessary.

The scene was etched forever in her mind.

CHAPTER SEVEN

"I want them to see what they have done."
Jacqueline Kennedy, November 22, 1963

It was chaos at the sheriff's department. After being led to the main desk, a harried clerk asked them to find a seat until someone could take their statements.

Kate looked around her at the frenetic activity. In one side office, she saw a crowd huddled in front of a television. A news crew carrying cameras burst through the front door with other reporters from the *Dallas News* and *The Times Herald* already on site and yelling out questions that everyone ignored. Telephones were ringing on every desk. All in all, it was a madhouse.

Frank Gallagher, his family close behind him, elbowed his way through the crowd to a vacant bench against the wall. There his family sat waiting to give their affidavits.

"Dad, see what's on the radio."

"Okay, son." Mr. Gallagher once again retrieved the radio from his pocket and turned on the local news station. Finding it impossible to hear in the surrounding din, he fished the earpiece from a pocket and reattached it to the small box. Once he hooked the earpiece over his outer ear, his expression took on a glazed look of concentration as he processed what he was hearing. "They're reporting from Parkland Hospital," he finally said, "but there's no official word yet on the president."

"Kate, do you think I should put the part about the man with the rifle in my report?" Danny inquired.

"Why wouldn't you?"

"Well, maybe someone will come after me for being a witness."

"You didn't see the man with the rifle actually shoot it, did you?"

"I might have," Danny mumbled.

"You might have?" Kate echoed back.

"Yeah, I looked back up there when I heard that first shot. I saw the same man with the gun pointing right down at us."

"Danny, you need to tell the truth. If you saw him firing the gun, then say so. There were other people besides us who saw him."

"But you said you weren't sure."

"I'm sure I saw a man up there with a rifle. I'm just not sure if he's the one who shot the president," Kate responded. "I just can't ... "

"Oh, no," groaned Frank Gallagher. "It's official. They just announced that the president died at 1:00 p.m. of a gunshot wound to the brain."

As her dad's eyes filled, Kate could see his Adam's apple bobbing up and down as he fought to maintain control.

Kate's mother began sobbing. Soon the sound of crying could be heard all over the room as word spread. Grown men stood with tears streaming down their cheeks while others slowly shook their heads in denial of what had occurred in their city.

Kate glanced at the wall clock and saw that it was 1:30. The president had already been dead a half hour.

In her heart of hearts, she had known that. No one could have survived that final gunshot. Kate shuddered as her mind replayed the bullet's impact. A terrible tightness filled her chest and a lump formed in her throat, but she couldn't cry.

Glancing over at Danny, she saw him staring at the floor. She grabbed his hand and squeezed, and, for once in his life, he didn't pull away.

Mr. Gallagher resumed monitoring the radio and kept reporting to the family as developments were announced. According to one of the doctors who attended the president, it was possible that one of the wounds had come from a shot to the front, indicating more than one gunman. This news seemed to reinforce her mother's belief that she had heard shots from up the embankment.

After what seemed like hours, the Gallaghers were finally ushered to a crowded office to give their statements. A tired-looking deputy interrogated each of them while a stenographer wrote out their responses. As Kate stood to leave the room, the officer noticed her camera. "Did you take pictures?"

"Yes, I took about six or seven."

"Of the shooting?" he inquired.

"No, I don't think so. I took some while we were waiting and then a couple when the motorcade started coming. I was just about to get a second picture of Mrs. Kennedy when the first shot happened. I'm not sure what I did then. My camera was on the ground when it was over."

"I need your film."

"Why? These are my pictures. I don't want to lose them." Kate's voice began to rise as she struggled to keep her composure.

Her father put his arm around her shoulders. "They need the pictures for evidence, Kate. Right, Officer?"

"Right. I just want the film; you can keep your camera. We can even give you a receipt for the film so you can get it later. We're asking everyone who has pictures to turn them over." He pointed to several rolls of film on the table behind them.

Kate sighed as she turned her camera over and began to rewind the partially exposed roll of film. She snapped open the film compartment and handed the roll to the outstretched hand. The deputy painstakingly wrote her name and the date on a piece of paper and taped it to the roll. "I'll get a receipt for you."

Kate's family returned to the bench and waited for their statements to be typed for signature. The battery was fading in her dad's radio, so he turned it off.

Kate stared at the clock on the wall and found herself thinking about her classmates. She'd been so caught up in the events here that she hadn't given a thought to what was going on elsewhere. Her friends would be in sixth period by now. Did they know about the president? Might school be dismissed early? She was supposed to go to a basketball game tonight. Would it still be held? Regardless, she knew she didn't feel like going.

Bystanders she recognized from Dealey Plaza were leaning against walls, sitting on benches or even on the floor waiting for their turns to give their statements. All of them looked tense and ill, as if they were recovering from the flu. A few spoke quietly, but most people just sat and stared.

Kate overhead one man urging his wife not to make a statement. He was certain their own lives could be in jeopardy if they did so. He'd heard reporters say there were rumors someone in the Secret Service had been killed and the vice president wounded.

Kate hadn't seen either of those things happen, but could there have been other attacks further down the route? Somehow that didn't seem likely, but, then, nothing made sense right now.

Time dragged, but eventually a clerk told them their accounts were ready to sign. When Kate returned to the deputy's office to proofread her statement, he had her receipt for the film ready as well. Each family member carefully read their typed affidavits, made corrections as needed, and added their signatures. It was almost 3:30 before they were finally told that they could leave.

"What happens now, Dad?" Danny asked as they made their way through the mob.

"I guess we wait to see if they contact us. We probably won't hear anything more, but it's possible we could be asked to testify later at a trial. But, I don't know what good that would do. None of us actually saw who did the shooting."

"I just want to go home, Frank."

Kate looked at her mother. She seemed to have shrunk over the course of the afternoon.

"Right. Let's get out of here."

Without another word they left.

CHAPTER EIGHT

"This is a sad time for all people.
We have suffered a loss that cannot be weighed."
Lyndon Johnson, Andrews Air Force Base,
November 22, 1963

When the Gallaghers stepped outside the county building, the streets were deserted except for the police activity still occurring in front of the Texas School Book Depository. As they walked the blocks to their parked car, they occasionally encountered a forlorn-looking individual. Once they passed a young black woman sitting on the curb sobbing. On another block, they walked by an appliance store where a small silent group sat watching a television playing in the window. It looked like a reporter was announcing from Parkland Hospital.

Kate turned from the sight. For just a few minutes, she wanted peace. She wanted to empty her mind of the horrible images it contained. She wanted to walk in silence and pretend this was just a normal day. Why was that so hard to do?

By the time their dad pulled the car into the driveway, it was growing dark. The ride home had passed quickly with each of them lost in their own thoughts. The radio station had been completely taken over by news bulletins giving details about the shooting, as they became known.

They exited the vehicle in unison and made their way into the house. Kate and Danny each headed for their rooms, wanting the comfort of familiar surroundings and prized belongings. Frank Gallagher walked around turning on lights in the living room, dining room, and kitchen in an attempt to bring some semblance of cheer to the gloomy silence.

He found his wife standing in the kitchen staring at the refrigerator. "Why don't you go lie down, Barbara? I can manage something for us to eat." She nodded and walked off without speaking. He inspected the contents of the refrigerator and was soon pulling out the makings of a light supper. Only Danny had eaten since breakfast. In spite of the circumstances, everyone needed something to eat.

In her room, Kate crawled under her comforter with her favorite stuffed animal under her arm. She felt chilled and nauseous. Over and over, the tragic scene at Dealey Plaza paraded through her mind. She wasn't surprised to hear a soft knock on her door a few minutes later. This was followed by Danny coming in and flopping down beside her. She noticed that his new sweater had already been replaced by the homey comfort of the old sweatshirt.

"What are you thinking, Kate?"

"I don't know. I guess I'm wondering what they'll find when they develop my film. I'm wondering if there's a lunatic on the loose and whether our country is falling apart."

"I'm wondering if they caught the killer," Danny replied. After a few minutes of shared silence, he gently prodded his sister. "Come on. It won't do any good to lie here; let's go turn on the TV and see if there's any more news."

"You go ahead. I want to change clothes first."

A few minutes later, clad in favorite slacks and a sweater, Kate wandered into the living room to find her dad and Danny watching the live news coverage from downtown Dallas. Much of the news was a recap of everything they had seen firsthand plus new details that were emerging from Parkland Hospital. They were surprised to learn that Governor Connally was undergoing surgery for his multiple gun wounds and was listed in grave condition. No one else had been wounded. That, at least, was good news.

"Come on into the kitchen, kids. I made grilled cheese sandwiches and tomato soup. I'm going to check on your mother."

"Dad, can we eat in the living room?"

"Why not? Get out the TV trays. I'll see if your mother will join us."

Kate and Danny set up four TV trays and went to the kitchen to put together plates. They carried their makeshift dinner back into the living room and turned up the volume on the television. National journalists had made their way to Dallas, and the reporter broadcasting live from Dealey Plaza was a familiar face.

"With no more than a hundred bystanders at this particular intersection, the eyewitness reports are scattered. Several bystanders who watched the motorcade from the grassy knoll report that gunshots were fired from the top of the incline toward the presidential limousine ..."

"Grassy knoll? Kate, does he mean where we stood? Is that the grassy knoll?"

"I think so. That's where he's pointing. Look! That's right where we were in front of the pavilion by those stairs," Kate said. "Dad called it an embankment, but it's the same place, a grassy knoll."

"What's going on?" Frank Gallagher asked as he joined his children.

"Where's Mom?" Danny asked.

"She's going to rest for a while. She has a headache. Anything new?" he asked as he sat down and picked up his sandwich.

"Yeah. They said some people think there were shots from the grassy knoll. See where that reporter's standing? It's right where we were," Danny explained. "That's the same place Mom thought she heard a shot coming from."

Television coverage continued, but soon the emphasis switched from the shooting to bulletins about a suspect being sought who worked at the Book Depository. Reporters interviewed several employees who gave descriptions of suspicious behavior by someone named Lee Harvey Oswald who had carried a long narrow package into work that morning.

The telephone rang, interrupting their concentration. Danny jumped up to answer it and came back saying, "Dad, it's Uncle Bob. He wants to talk to you."

Frank Gallagher quickly walked into the kitchen to take the long distance call from his brother who lived in Illinois. Kate and Danny could hear snatches of the conversation as their dad relayed a synopsis of what the family had experienced.

Mr. Gallagher had barely hung up and started back to the living room when the phone rang a second time. This time the call was from their aunt and uncle who lived a couple of hours outside Dallas.

That call was followed by one from their paternal grandparents. It seemed that everyone in the family remembered the Gallaghers had been on hand for the motorcade, and now they wanted a firsthand report.

It wasn't ten minutes after her grandparents hung up that Kate received her first telephone call. Judy wanted details about where she had been standing and what she had seen, but Kate wasn't up to rehashing her experience. "I just can't talk about it right now, Judy. I'm sorry, but I just can't. Not yet."

"Did you see it happen?" Judy persisted.

"Yes. Maybe later I will tell you about it, but not right now. I have to go."

"Are you going to the ballgame tonight?"

Kate made a disgusted sound. "No, of course not. How can you even ask?"

"What about tomorrow? Are you still going to Brenda's slumber party?" Judy asked. "You've got to go to that."

"She's still having it?" Kate asked in amazement. "No, I won't be going."

The last thing Kate could imagine herself doing was sitting around giggling and gossiping with her friends while the president of the United States lay in his coffin.

"I think she's still having it; I haven't heard that it's called off."

"Well, I can't believe anyone would feel like a party after the president has been killed," mumbled Kate. "Look, I need to go. I'll talk to you later."

Kate hung up the phone and walked back in to join her dad and Danny. "If anyone else calls for me, tell them I don't want to talk."

"What's wrong, Kate?" Danny wanted to know.

"Oh, nothing." Kate sighed. "Just Judy wanting to know if I'm still going to Brenda's slumber party. Can you believe that?"

"I guess this tragedy hasn't hit everyone the way it has us," Kate's dad offered. "The reality of it probably hasn't hit home yet."

"What hasn't hit home yet?" Kate's mom asked as she walked into the room. Her eyes were red, and she looked like she was recovering from an illness.

"Hi, Mom. Are you feeling any better? We were just talking about a phone call I had from Judy. She wanted a blow-by-blow account, but I told her I'm not ready to talk about it yet."

"I know. I'm still absorbing it myself. I know what my eyes saw, but it's like my brain can't believe it's real. I keep thinking I'll wake up and this will all be a horrible dream, a nightmare." Barbara Gallagher took a seat on the couch and turned her attention to the television while her husband went to the kitchen to fix her something to eat.

" ... *NBC has just learned that police arrested Lee Harvey Oswald at 2:00 this afternoon after apprehending him at the Texas Theater. Oswald is being held on one charge of murder in the slaying of Dallas police officer J. D. Tippit. Witnesses say that Oswald shot the officer as he attempted to stop and question him. Oswald is also the prime suspect in the assassination of President Kennedy. At this time he is being questioned by Secret Service and FBI interrogators.*"

"They reported earlier that Oswald worked at the Book Depository. Do you think he could be the man with the rifle we saw in the window?" Danny turned to look at Kate.

"I don't know. I don't think I could recognize anyone. I saw him so fast ... All I'm sure of is that it was a man," Kate responded.

She glanced back at the television screen where they were now showing a list of all the local evening and weekend events that had been canceled in respect for the slain president. Other than for a rare snow day, she had never known so many events to be called off.

Next the television network switched to live scenes from Andrews Air Force Base in Washington, D.C. It was already dark on the East Coast, but live coverage showed that a small crowd of government officials and a large mob of reporters were standing on the tarmac waiting while the large plane taxied to a stop. First a set of rolling stairs was pushed into place in front of the plane's door, and then a forklift was driven to the rear of the plane.

Bobby Kennedy, the president's brother as well as a cabinet member, quickly walked up the stairs and disappeared into the plane. The television announcer's tone was soft and somber as he described the scene for the viewers. The crowd waited patiently for the first lady to emerge and come down the stairs while a camera zoomed in on the activity at the rear of the plane where the forklift was being used to remove the casket.

"Look at that; Jacqueline Kennedy still has on the same clothes she wore when we saw her," Kate commented. She struggled with more raw emotion as she watched the president's coffin being taken off *Air Force One*.

Behind the coffin, a somber Mrs. Kennedy clutched the hand of her brother-in-law. Her dazed, stone-like expression was testament to the grief frozen within her.

The coffin was loaded into a waiting hearse to be driven to Bethesda Naval Hospital where an official autopsy would be conducted, and both Mrs. Kennedy and her brother-in-law departed in an official car making its way to the hospital.

Lyndon Baines Johnson and his wife Lady Bird descended the steps of the plane once the hearse had departed. LBJ was now the thirty-sixth president of the United States. He had taken the oath of office on board *Air Force One* as he stood beside his wife and Mrs. Kennedy. He was the first president ever to be sworn in by a woman, and he was the first president ever to assume office just a few yards from the body of his predecessor.

The events of this day were continuing to provide more and more material for the history books, Kate reflected.

She and her family spent the evening fielding phone calls from relatives and friends. They silently watched the ongoing television reports until it became clear that no new developments were occurring. Finally, a saturation level was reached. Without much discussion, the television was turned off. Kate helped carry plates and bowls into the kitchen. She and her mother washed and dried the few dishes while her dad and Danny folded the TV trays. Completely drained by the emotional toll the day had taken, they all went to their rooms.

Kate had not been able to get warm since the shooting had occurred. She dug a warm flannel nightgown out of her drawer and changed quickly. She turned out the light and crawled into bed, pulling the thick comforter up to her chin. Fatigue rolled over her, and she welcomed the oblivion of sleep.

CHAPTER NINE

"I haven't shot anybody."
Lee Harvey Oswald, November 22, 1963

K ate opened her eyes and saw that it was still dark. Saturday. She could turn over and go back to sleep. Then the dark monster that had eluded her all night suddenly hurdled back into her consciousness with full force.

The shooting.

For a very few precious seconds, she had forgotten. She had almost convinced herself this was a normal weekend. She had hoped to awaken and find the horrible events of yesterday a bad dream, but, instead, a tidal wave of regret and sadness washed over her.

If only she could turn back the clock twenty-four hours. If only she and Danny had reported seeing the man with the rifle. If only the shooter had merely wounded the president. If only ...

After playing the "If Only" game for a while, Kate decided to get up. She couldn't sleep, and she was tired of lying in bed. She slowly pulled back the covers and slid to a sitting position. With a stretch and a yawn, she stood up and pulled on some socks and a warm bathrobe before heading to the bathroom.

No one else was up, so Kate went back to her bedroom and turned on a lamp. She made a conscious effort to cheer herself up. First, she turned on her radio and tuned it to her favorite station. She was relieved to hear the strains of one of her favorite Beach Boys songs rather than another news report. She hummed along in an attempt to think sunnier thoughts.

Then Kate went to her closet and dug out her scrapbook. Maybe it would help if she remembered the president in better days. She opened the cover to examine the clippings and magazine pictures she'd been saving since John Kennedy had run in the primaries three years ago. She sat on the bed and took her time looking through an assortment of pictures showing him campaigning, during his two and a half years in office, and spending time with his family.

That thick wavy hair and broad smile were his trademarks. He had been such a young and nice looking president, quite a change after the grandfatherly

Eisenhower. He'd had a special magnetism about him. What was that word? Charisma, Kate decided. The president has—the president had—charisma.

Then there was Jacqueline Bouvier Kennedy. How could you not admire her? She had researched the history of the White House and supervised its careful remodeling and restoration, and even the press agreed that she was the most stunning and elegant first lady in history. Her style had become the fashion setter for women everywhere. Kate had some good pictures of the first lady, but her favorite was the one taken on her wedding day.

Kate also had pictures of the two young Kennedy children, Caroline and John Jr. She loved the picture of little John-John hiding under the president's desk, a typical toddler. She turned the page to study a touching picture of the president playing with his young son, and a tightness filled her chest. Time to put the scrapbook away.

Kate gathered up some clothes and headed to the bathroom for a shower. By the time she emerged, the rest of her family was up and gathered in the kitchen. Danny was sitting at the table sorting through the larger than usual morning paper. While her mother took dishes out of the cabinet, her dad stood at the counter mixing up his special pancakes. It was a weekend tradition, and Kate knew he was going out of his way to bring some normalcy back into their lives. If she didn't know better, she could pretend this was just another weekend...

"Look at this headline, Dad." Danny held up the paper. "It says they've now arrested this Oswald guy for the shooting."

"Anything in there on the governor?" Barbara Gallagher asked.

Danny rummaged through the first couple of pages until he found an article reporting that the governor had come through a successful surgery and was expected to fully recover.

"That's one good thing anyway," their mother responded.

Danny continued to read tidbits out of the *Dallas News* while Kate set the table. Soon they were each sitting down to a plate of steaming pancakes. As they were finishing up their breakfast, the phone rang. It was Brenda for Kate.

"Hello."

"Kate, I'm just calling to make sure you're still coming tonight. Judy said you were acting funny."

"I'm sorry, Brenda. I'm just not in the mood for a party. I know it will be wonderful, but I'm not very good company right now."

"You're really being selfish, Kate Gallagher! I thought we were friends, and friends don't break promises!"

The phone slammed down in Kate's ear.

Kate stood fixated on the receiver for a long moment before hanging up.

"What was that all about, Kate?" her mother wanted to know.

"Brenda hung up on me. She's furious because I'm not coming to her slumber party." Kate's voice trailed off as she stared out the window, lost in her own thoughts.

"You know, maybe you should go. Brenda is one of your close friends, and it might do you some good to get out. Staying here won't change anything, you know," her mother said. "Don't decide now; just think about it."

By mutual agreement, the family members decided to leave the television turned off for the morning. Kate had her weekend dusting job to do, and Danny was slated to help his dad rake leaves. Kate's mother sat down at the table to put together her weekend grocery list.

"When you're at the supermarket, see if they have any other newspapers," Mr. Gallagher requested. "I want to try to buy all the different ones we can find and save them. Like it or not, this is a significant chapter in American history."

◆◆◆◆◆◆◆◆◆

Kate dusted the entire house as she did every Saturday. By the time she had also scoured the bathroom sink and tub, her mother had returned from the grocery store with several bags of groceries. As they unpacked and put everything away, the two of them deliberately avoided the tragedy and talked about routine things.

"Mom, I don't have my books from school. I'm supposed to have a science test on Monday, and I don't have my notes. I also don't have my math book."

"First of all, there won't be any school Monday. I heard on the radio that Monday has been declared a national day of mourning. President Kennedy's funeral is being broadcast live. Also, I think your teachers will understand. You had no idea you wouldn't get back to school for your afternoon classes. Maybe you could borrow one of your friend's math books so you could copy the problems down."

That was a good suggestion. Kate telephoned Judy who only lived two blocks away. Judy was happy to let her come over and copy the problems, so Kate located some notebook paper and left for her friend's house.

Judy opened the front door before Kate could even ring the doorbell. "Are you all right, Kate?"

Kate nodded. "I'm all right, I guess. I had terrible nightmares, but I can't exactly remember them. I just feel like I'm walking through a fog. I keep pushing the images away, or I wouldn't be able to get anything done."

Judy took Kate to her room, where she already had the algebra book open to the page of problems. Kate started copying them down, leaving several lines between them so she could work them out later. One thing about Mrs. Tinberg, she made them show all their work.

"Did you see the shooting?" Judy suddenly asked, interrupting Kate's train of thought.

"Yes. I saw the whole awful thing. At first I thought it was just a firecracker, but then there was a second shot and people started running and screaming. But the third shot ... The third shot was the worst. It's the one I can't get out of my mind." Kate sighed and continued to copy the equations. "I don't want to talk about it anymore right now, Judy."

"What did Jackie do?" Judy spoke as though she hadn't heard Kate. She had never been a fan of the president, but she adored the intriguing first lady.

"What do you think she did?" Kate was disgusted with her friend's morbid curiosity, especially since she knew that Judy didn't mourn the president as she did.

"She was frozen in shock and covered in blood. Is that what you want to hear?"

"I just want to know; you don't have to get mad. What's wrong with you?"

"What's wrong with me? I just saw our president slaughtered in front of my eyes, and you want to know how his wife took it." Kate shut the algebra book and stood to leave. "Thanks. I've got to go."

"But you're coming to Brenda's tonight, aren't you?"

"I don't know yet. I told my mom I'd think about it. I'll see how I feel."

"You've got to come, Kate. Everyone will be there." Judy followed Kate, who was heading for the bedroom door.

"Thanks for letting me use your book," Kate repeated. She didn't want to be rude, but she couldn't wait to get out of there.

Kate took her time walking home, puzzled over Judy's reaction to the president's death. Never had Judy expressed any sorrow or words of regret, and Kate just couldn't understand it. She wondered if she herself would have been that callous if a different candidate had won the election only to be assassinated later. "I hope I never act like that," she thought.

***

Later that afternoon, the Gallaghers were seated in the living room around the television set once again. After sticking to their agreement to avoid watching any TV in the morning, they were now eager to catch up on the latest developments. They learned that a large state funeral was being planned for Monday for the slain leader. Many of the details were being modeled after the funeral of President Abraham Lincoln, which had occurred nearly a century earlier.

During the wee hours of Friday night, the president's body had been prepared and brought to the East Room of the White House where it was being guarded by a Death Watch. President John Fitzgerald Kennedy was the sixth president whose body had occupied that room in death. There he remained all of Saturday while the Kennedy family, close friends, and cabinet members traveled through rain-drenched Washington to pay their respects.

After a lengthy debate between Robert and Jackie Kennedy, it had been decided that the coffin would remain closed. It was best for the country to remember John Kennedy as the vibrant and energetic man he had been rather than the waxy form left behind.

The networks also showed how the world at large was reacting to the news of the young president's death. Berliners gathered and carried torches through the streets. Kennedy had visited their country in the spring, and the Germans felt a special regard for him. Flags flew at half-staff in London, people prayed in Korea, and even the newspapers in Moscow gave the story front page coverage.

Kate couldn't help but note that many of the world's citizens were showing more grief and dismay than her own classmates.

Tired of the repetitious news stories, Kate went to her room to tackle the algebra problems she had copied from Judy's book. She took out the notebook paper and skimmed over the twenty equations, noting they didn't seem any harder than the ones they'd been doing in class the past week. She cleared some space at her desk and began working her way through them. She was very good at math and found some satisfaction in completing the problems. It was nice to feel in control of something.

After finishing the assignment, Kate stretched out on her bed with the radio playing softly in the background. Should she go to Brenda's slumber party? She was torn. On the one hand, the events of yesterday made the thought of a slumber party seem silly and even disrespectful. Why should teenaged girls laugh and have fun while the Kennedy family struggled to deal with a travesty that had occurred right here in her hometown?

On the other hand, she was tired of sitting around. Neither her friends nor the city of Dallas were to blame for the assassination; it could have happened anywhere. And Kate was becoming restless. Normally she was on the go, and the inactivity of the weekend was starting to wear on her.

Then there was the issue of Brenda herself. While she wasn't her best friend, she certainly was a key member of the group Kate ran around with. If Brenda got down on her, the repercussions would be felt for days, maybe even weeks. After her absence from the slumber party kicked in, she could picture Brenda phoning friend after friend to gossip about Kate and belittle her for grieving over JFK. Some of the girls were resentful as it was because Kate was popular and earned such good grades. They'd be more than happy to join Brenda in making Kate's life miserable. Sometimes being fourteen could be such a pain. Kate continued to wrestle with the decision. To go or not to go?

CHAPTER TEN

"A bad man shot my daddy."
John-John Kennedy, November 23, 1963

Barbara Gallagher knocked on her daughter's door. "Kate, can I come in?"

"Sure."

Her mother walked in and sat down on the bed. "What have you decided about the party?"

"I guess I haven't decided. I really don't want to go, but I feel like I should, and that makes me mad. I know I promised Brenda I'd be there, but that was before everything else happened. I just wish she would postpone this."

"I know, but evidently she isn't going to. I think you should go, Kate. You've been around here all day, and nothing is going to happen tonight. We'll pick you up tomorrow for Mass and then we'll come home and watch the televised memorial tribute. Monday, you'll have the whole day to watch the funeral."

"Yeah, I guess you're right." Kate stood up and smiled at her mother. "I'd better get ready. Thanks, Mom." She hugged her mother and turned to retrieve her overnight bag from the closet.

After Kate changed clothes and cleaned up, she finished packing the small overnight bag. Danny came into her room to watch. "I wish I had something to do. All they're showing on TV is the same thing over and over. Mostly stuff about Oswald being a Communist."

"I know. I don't really want to go, but it will be nice to get out." Kate shut the lid of her small overnight case and looked at her watch. "I guess I'd better take off."

Her father drove her to Brenda's house, and Danny rode along for something to do. Because her feelings for her brother had shifted in the past twenty-four hours, Kate even let him sit up front since she'd be getting out of the car soon anyway.

"Try to have a good time, honey. You need to relax." Her father spoke as he pulled the car to a stop in front of the large colonial house where the Gleasons lived.

"Okay, Dad, I'll try." Kate kissed him good-bye and got out of the car. "Bye, Danny." Still a bit reluctant to join the festivities, she watched her dad drive away before turning and heading up the sidewalk.

She lifted the large brass knocker on the front door and was welcomed by Brenda's mother.

"Why, Kate. We weren't sure you were going to make it. Brenda will be so happy that you came. Just put your bag down here. The girls are all downstairs in the rec room."

Kate didn't need any help finding the stairs to the recreation room; the loud music and laughing were beacon enough. She made her way slowly down the stairs feeling hesitant about joining the others. She took a deep breath and tried to put on her party face.

"Kate! You made it!" Judy rushed over and linked her arm through Kate's. "I was hoping you would come. Brenda's dad has gone to get the pizzas, but there's chips and dip over here."

She ushered Kate to where the snacks were located, and they both stood eating as they surveyed the group of a dozen girls, several of whom were dancing to "Louie, Louie" as others sang along. Brenda was busy chasing her younger sister and brother out of the room. After she managed to get them up the stairs, she came back and noticed Kate for the first time. For some reason, she made a point of ignoring her.

"Okay, that's the way it's going to be," Kate thought to herself. "The cold shoulder." She turned away and resumed watching the others. The song had ended, and Gail was braiding Darla's hair as they gossiped and joked. Two other girls were huddled over a note from a boyfriend. Brenda's cat was running between the furniture looking for a place to hide. All in all, it appeared to be a pretty typical slumber party.

Kate managed to keep a low profile as the girls ate pizza and chatted. She found her own tension easing when no one confronted her about the assassination. She had the feeling that Judy had warned them to steer clear of that topic, and she was grateful to her friend.

Later, when things started to slow down a bit, Terrie suggested they play charades. Two teams were formed, and the antics began to a background of cheering and horsing around. When it was time for Kate to draw her phrase out of the basket, Gail called out, "Hey, Kate, why don't you pantomime the assassination for us?"

Only one or two of the others looked uncomfortable; the rest laughed uproariously.

Kate was astonished. As tears sprang unwittingly to her eyes, she spun on her heels and ran up the stairs.

"Kate, wait!" shouted Judy.

Brenda came chasing up the stairs after her as Kate rushed into the front foyer and looked around for the overnight case she'd left there.

"Where are you going?" Brenda confronted Kate just as her mother came in from the kitchen.

"Girls, what's going on?" asked Mrs. Gleason.

"Mom, Kate is leaving. She can't leave just because someone made a stupid joke," Brenda insisted.

"A joke? You think it's funny to joke about the president's death?" Kate angrily brushed away the tears that were coursing down her cheeks.

Mrs. Gleason smiled in a condescending manner. "Kate, dear. You know that none of us supported Mr. Kennedy. Don't be so sensitive. Go back downstairs to the party."

Kate had been raised to treat adults with respect and dared not respond, but she was too angry at Gail's so-called joke and at Mrs. Gleason's attitude to stay. "May I use the phone to call my dad?" she asked.

Mrs. Gleason blinked with surprise. "Why, of course you can use the phone, Kate, but I wish you'd reconsider. Brenda has been planning this party for a long time."

Kate shook her head and walked over to the telephone on the hall table. After dialing her home number, she spoke softly into the receiver. Brenda gave her a dirty look and stomped back downstairs to the party.

"Thank you, Mrs. Gleason. I think I'll wait on the front porch." Kate picked up her bag and went outside.

She started down the steps when she saw her dad approaching. She had the car door open even before he had come to a complete stop.

"Kate, what's wrong?"

"I just want to go home, Dad. I never should have come."

Mr. Gallagher sensed that it was better to forego the questioning for now. An explanation would come later. They drove home in silence.

Kate had already unpacked her overnight bag and put it away when her father knocked on the door and asked to come in. She noticed that Danny, too, slipped in. He sat on the bed without saying anything.

"Want to tell me what happened?" Mr. Gallagher knew his level-headed daughter was not usually one for hysterics, so the fact that she'd left the party so abruptly meant something had really upset her.

Kate sat down at her desk. "It was awful. I shouldn't have gone, but I felt like Brenda would be mad if I didn't."

"So what did Brenda do?"

"It wasn't actually Brenda. Well, in a way it was. When I first got there only Judy acted happy to see me. Brenda wasn't speaking to me, but I just ignored her. Then we ate and listened to records—just fooled around. I was starting to feel better, like it was going to be okay after all. Then we played charades." Kate then described Gail's ugly comment.

"Gosh, that's … "

"Danny, let Kate finish. Go on; what happened then?" Mr. Gallagher asked.

"The worst part was Mrs. Gleason. Gail always acts like a jerk, so I can't be too surprised at anything she says, but I never dreamed Mrs. Gleason could be like that. She said they never voted for Kennedy and I shouldn't be so sensitive! Can you believe that, Dad? She acted almost glad that the president had been killed because they hadn't wanted him to be president in the first place."

No one said anything for a minute.

"I guess I see why you wanted to come home," her dad finally said. "I can't believe the Gleasons are glad the president was murdered, but it was a terrible thing to say. If anyone is out of line, it's her, Kate, not you. I guess some people just let their political leanings cloud their thinking. My guess is that someday Mrs. Gleason will look back on that scene and be embarrassed by her behavior."

"I never liked Brenda anyway. She's thinks she's so cool," Danny added.

"Well, I don't think you'll have to worry about her, Danny. I doubt she'll be coming over here anymore," Kate continued. "In fact, I don't know if anyone will want to be friends with me after tonight."

"Those kinds of friends you can do without, honey. But give it some time. Some of them will come around. They just don't see the big picture yet." Frank Gallagher stood up and gave his daughter a big hug. "Your mom went to bed early, but Danny and I were getting ready to set up the Scrabble board. Come on; let's see if I can beat you guys."

In spite of her sorrow over the president and the fiasco at the sleeping party, Kate grinned. There really was no place like home.

CHAPTER ELEVEN

"You killed the President, you rat!"
Jack Ruby, November 24, 1963

"Kate, it's time to get up."

She forced her eyes open, surprised to see that her room was bright with sunlight. After hours of tossing and turning, she had apparently managed to drop off to sleep.

"Okay, Mom. I'm getting up." Kate hurried out of bed and grabbed her bathrobe.

She found her family in the kitchen where her mother was just setting a platter of blueberry muffins on the table. On mornings when they went to early Mass, they didn't eat a big breakfast.

"You must have slept well."

Kate didn't respond; it was better that her mother not know about the dark thoughts that had kept her awake most of the night. Her mother turned to the counter to pour two cups of coffee. "Your dad told me about the party. I'm sorry; I guess my advice wasn't so good after all."

"It's not your fault." Kate reached for a muffin and began buttering it. She nodded at her dad and Danny dividing up the sections of the large Sunday newspaper. "Anything new in the paper?"

Before Frank Gallagher could answer, the telephone rang and Kate's mother answered it.

"Oh, hello, Cindy." Barbara Gallagher spoke to her sister for a few minutes, updating her on events since their husbands had spoken Friday night. "Yes, we plan to be home except for going to church this morning. We'd love to have you." She continued making plans for several minutes before hanging up. It was the first time in two days that Kate had heard any enthusiasm in her mother's voice.

"Cindy, Dave, and the boys want to drive down this afternoon and spend the night with us. They thought it might be nice for all of us to watch the funeral together tomorrow," Kate's mother explained. "I think they want to be around family."

"Oh, boy!" said Danny with enthusiasm. He and Kate both enjoyed spending time with their two cousins. They didn't get to see them that often since they lived several hours away. Scott was a year older than Kate and Jeff a year younger than Danny.

"It will be nice to have them here. There's a memorial service scheduled for this afternoon." Frank Gallagher drank his coffee and began sharing updates from the morning paper. He glanced at the kitchen clock and hastily folded the paper.

"Okay, kids, scoot," he said. "Time to get dressed for church; we need to leave in twenty minutes."

Kate hurried to her room to get ready, looking forward to seeing her relatives. It would be a welcome change of pace.

Mass was well attended, especially for the early service. Kate wondered why it took holidays and tragedies to compel people to attend, but after the unexplainable events of Friday, she supposed many were turning to church seeking solace and comfort.

As she participated in the routine ritual, Kate couldn't help but reflect on the sadness permeating the air. Many of the parishioners had supported Kennedy's election and felt a special kinship to the first lady. Monsignor's homily dealt with the assassination, of course, as he talked about the need for the country to come together during this difficult time of national mourning. Kate couldn't help but wish that the girls from the slumber party were sitting beside her, but she doubted it would have done much good anyway.

When church was over, she followed her parents into the community room where people gathered between services for coffee and cookies. Several of her parents' friends made a point of talking to them about the president's death and were astounded to hear that the Gallaghers had been witnesses at Dealey Plaza. Each of her parents retold their experiences over and over.

"You mean you were right there on the grassy knoll?" Kate heard her dad launch into another abbreviated version of what had transpired on Friday. Not wanting to hear the story yet again, Kate wandered over to get some lemonade and join some of the kids near her in age.

"Oswald is a Commie," she heard one of the boys comment. "Just wait 'til his trial. It'll take hundreds of cops to protect him!"

"Yeah, he'll be lucky to make it to trial without someone gunning him down," added another teenager.

Kate could not keep silent. "Surely you don't think someone will try to kill Oswald?"

"Why not? It would sure save the taxpayers a lot of time and money. I bet a lot of people just wish someone would take Oswald out!"

Kate shook her head in disbelief. "I can't believe you really think that. Don't you want to know what happened, the whole story? How do you even know if Oswald acted alone?"

Another girl chimed in, agreeing with Kate. "My dad thinks Oswald was probably working for Castro. It's probably a conspiracy."

And so the debate went on as a half dozen teenagers volunteered their perspectives on why anyone would want to kill the young president. Kate was relieved when Danny came to tell her their parents were ready to leave.

After getting home and changing into comfortable clothes, Danny and Kate set up a card table and jigsaw puzzle in the living room. They thought their cousins would enjoy having something to do as they watched the television broadcast. Danny switched on the TV so they could learn if there were any new details. According to the morning paper, Oswald was still adamantly denying that he had killed anyone, yet ballistics tests had already proven that the rifle found at the Texas School Book Depository bearing his finger-prints was indeed the weapon used in the assassination. And eyewitnesses had positively identified Oswald as the man who had shot J. D. Tippit, the police officer who was killed about forty-five minutes after the assassination of President Kennedy. In spite of the mounting evidence, Oswald had not confessed.

Kate opened a thousand-piece jigsaw puzzle box and began arranging the pieces on the table. She glanced up at the television scene and learned that NBC had live coverage of the Dallas police transferring Lee Harvey Oswald from the city prison to the county jail. The TV camera picked up the scene as Oswald emerged from an elevator into the basement of the jail. With a detective on each side, Oswald looked defiant, his hands cuffed in front of him.

"Kate, look. Oswald has a black eye." Danny pointed toward the screen, and Kate nodded as her brother continued, "Wonder how he got that?"

The police continued to escort Oswald through a hallway toward a waiting armored vehicle that would transport him to his new cell. Surprisingly, reporters and onlookers were lining the basement area and nothing had been done to protect the prisoner.

Suddenly, a burly figure rushed forward with his arm outstretched and fired a single shot straight at Oswald's chest.

"Oh my gosh!" yelled Danny.

Kate gasped. "Dad! Mom! Come quick!"

Both of their parents rushed into the room.

"What is it, son?" Frank Gallagher practically shouted the question as he glanced at Kate's white face and then turned his attention to the television screen where confusion reigned.

Oswald had already dropped to the floor. The television camera continued to roll, showing millions of viewers the skirmish between the police and the man who had just shot the president's accused assassin.

Barbara Gallagher dropped onto the couch with a look of astonishment. "What's going on? What happened?"

"That man in the hat, he shot Oswald. He just walked right up to him and fired!" Danny told her.

The police now had the assailant cuffed. They dragged him out of camera range while others mobbed the fallen Oswald.

For the next half hour, the four Gallaghers silently watched the drama unfold on live television. Oswald was lifted onto a gurney and rolled out to a waiting ambulance. In an eerie flashback to Friday, reporters once again flocked to the emergency entrance of Parkland Hospital. Oswald's unconscious form was whisked through the doors while NBC recounted the shooting and said the condition of the victim appeared to be critical.

Meanwhile, another reporter still covering the scene in the basement at the jailhouse said the assailant had been identified as one Jack Ruby. Ruby was known by police as the owner of a sleazy Dallas nightclub. No motive for the shooting had been determined yet.

"I can't believe this. What is wrong with people? I can't believe I live in a country where this is happening." Barbara Gallagher continued to ramble as her husband looked on helplessly and patted her hand.

"It was awful. He just walked right up and shot him. The police just stood there," Kate said in disbelief.

At that moment, the doorbell rang. Frank Gallagher rose from the couch to answer it. "Come in, come in. Did you hear what happened? We're in the living room."

Cindy McDonald walked quickly into the living room and took a look at her sister's stricken face. "Barbara? What's going on?"

Barbara Gallagher stood up and embraced her sister as she began to sob.

Dave McDonald and his sons were just entering the front door with overnight bags, pillows, and some covered dishes.

"Hi, Frank. What's up?" Dave looked confused as he took in the scene before him.

Scott and Jeff set down the bags and walked over to their cousins.

"Some guy named Jack Ruby just shot Oswald on live television. The kids saw the whole thing. We're waiting to hear if Oswald is going to make it. He looked pretty bad."

Scott turned to his cousins. "You saw it? What happened?" Kate narrated the scene she and Danny had just witnessed while Danny interjected his comments and opinions. Then he pointed to the TV.

"Look. They're showing it again." Everyone stopped talking and watched in horror as NBC replayed the shooting from the jailhouse.

"Man. This is just what Dallas doesn't need, more bad publicity. I can't believe they didn't do a better job of protecting Oswald." Dave McDonald shook his head in disgust. "He was a sitting duck."

"You know what the worst thing is?"

Everyone turned to look at Kate.

"If Oswald dies, we'll never know for sure who killed Kennedy."

CHAPTER TWELVE

"We're going to go say good-bye to Daddy, and we're going to kiss him good-bye ... "
Jacqueline Kennedy, Capitol Rotunda, November 24, 1963

Kate was glad her cousins were here. As the kids sat at the kitchen table eating sandwiches, they rehashed the events of the past forty-eight hours.

"Where were you when you first heard the news?" Kate asked Scott, a freshman in high school.

"I had just finished lunch and was on my way to class. Mr. Bowman was standing at the door and told us the president had been shot. No one believed him, and he got really mad. We thought it was some sort of joke at first, but then they started playing the radio over the school intercom. They kept it on until the announcement came that Kennedy was dead. You could have heard a pin drop. I've never heard the school so quiet."

"Then what happened?"

"Some of the kids started crying, even some of the boys. A bunch of kids asked if they could use the phone to call home. I even saw a few kids just get up and leave. No one stopped them."

"What did you do?" Kate was curious to see if Scott and his friends had taken the assassination as lightly as some of her friends had.

"I just started feeling kind of sick. I wasn't sure what to do, so I just sat there. Mr. Bowman didn't even try to have class. About twenty minutes later they announced that they were dismissing school early, so I walked home." Scott shook his head as if he could still somehow deny the events.

"My teacher cried," Jeff told them. He was ten years old and in the fifth grade. "We were having art and someone knocked on the door to talk to Miss Kravich. She started crying and everyone wanted to know what was wrong. Then she told us the president had been shot. I didn't know you were there, though. That must have really been awful. What was it like?"

"I saw a man with a rifle." Danny explained how he and Kate had thought the figure in the window was a Secret Service agent. "I wish now we'd told someone."

"You want to know something? Our high school football game wasn't even canceled. We're in the play-offs, so they went ahead and had the game, but I didn't go," Scott told them. "I just didn't feel up to it. I just sat home all night watching TV."

"Yeah, we did too. We watched all the news coverage, especially when they talked about the grassy knoll. We were standing right there. Danny and I went down close to the street, but Mom and Dad were higher up on the hillside. They hit the ground after the first shot, so they didn't see everything like we did."

Kate described the first two shots to Jeff and Scott. Since they seemed genuinely interested, she described the third shot and how no one could have survived it.

"I've had nightmares about it," Danny mumbled.

"You have? Why didn't you tell me?" Kate asked. She didn't remember her dreams, but she knew she hadn't been sleeping well either.

"I keep seeing this man chasing me with a rifle. Then when I turn around, he's laughing and he shoots the gun, but roses come out of it. It's weird."

Kate nodded and reached out to place her hand on Danny's arm. Only someone who had seen what they had witnessed could understand exactly how horrible it had been. Danny was just a kid, but he had seen something few adults would ever observe.

"Why would anyone want to shoot the president?" Jeff looked to the older kids for answers.

"I don't know. Maybe Oswald is just crazy." Kate knew that wasn't much of an answer.

"Or maybe it was a plot and Oswald was only part of it," Scott speculated. "Let's see if there's anything new on TV."

The kids left the kitchen and returned to the living room. They sat around the card table and began assembling the outside edge of the puzzle as they monitored the news. All they learned was that Oswald was undergoing emergency surgery.

Television coverage switched from Dallas to Washington, D.C. where it was an hour later. It was a little after 1:00 there when the deceased thirty-fifth president of the United States departed the White House for the last time. The procession to the capitol was watched by thousands lining the street as a caisson pulled by six white horses made its way up Pennsylvania Avenue.

Although police locked arms to form a barrier behind the cortege, their efforts were futile. There was no holding back the tidal wave of bystanders. Silently the crowd pushed through the blockade and fell into place behind the procession. Thousands followed the cortege in respectful silence until it reached the east front of the capitol. There the Navy Band playing "Hail to the Chief" followed a twenty-one-gun salute. The music was the undoing of Kate's mother and aunt.

Both women sobbed softly as they watched the haunting scene.

Viewers got their first look at Jacqueline Kennedy since Friday night. Dressed completely in black, the first lady's face was expressionless. She had a child on each side of her as she ascended the east steps of the capitol behind the pallbearers. Inside the large rotunda, the president's coffin was lowered onto the same catafalque used for Lincoln's funeral. A single wreath was displayed at the foot of the dais while the five-man military honor guard stood at attention. Several hundred dignitaries ringed the flag-draped coffin. Little John-John Kennedy was a typical, restless toddler, so when he began to squirm, a Secret Service man took him outside. Five-year-old Caroline remained poised by her mother's side during the three eulogies.

"She has so much elegance and style," commented Aunt Cindy as they watched Senator Mike Mansfield deliver his tribute to the slain leader. Supreme Court Chief Justice Warren and Speaker of the House McCormack followed, giving their brief remarks.

"It's just so sad," commented Barbara Gallagher, "for her to bury a baby in August and now to lose her husband." No one answered since all of them were fighting their own wars with emotion. They continued to watch as President Johnson stepped forward to place a large floral tribute near the coffin.

But it was the next scene that was the breaking point for Kate. As the brief ceremony drew to a close, Jacqueline Kennedy took the hand of her small daughter and led her to the coffin. Together they knelt in front of the casket. The first lady leaned forward to brush her lips against the flag as the small, gloved hand of the child patted the coffin in a gesture of good-bye.

"Oh my gosh," mumbled Scott, his eyes brimming with tears.

Kate jumped up and ran from the room as the sobbing of her mother became louder. She could hardly see her way to her bedroom as her eyes filled and her throat thickened. She closed the door behind her and threw herself on the bed. Breathing deeply and forcing herself to think of something other than the simple majesty of the first lady, Kate was able to eventually bring her breathing back to normal. She knew she'd feel better if she could cry it out, but she couldn't. As the painful lump in her throat gradually dissolved, she stared at the ceiling and wondered for the hundredth time why anyone would want to take the life of the nation's president.

A short while later, Danny knocked softly on the door. He opened it a few inches, peered in, and entered the room. "Kate? Are you okay? Dad said to tell you that we're turning the TV off for a while. Everyone's had all they can take."

"Yeah, I'm okay. It's just so sad. But you know what? No matter how awful I feel, I can't cry. I wish I could, but I can't. My throat just closes up. I feel like I can't breathe, but the tears are locked up somewhere." Kate stood up and walked over to her dresser mirror to survey her face. She ran a brush through her hair and turned back to Danny. "Where are Scott and Jeff?"

"They're waiting for you to come back out."

Kate nodded and took a deep breath. "Okay. Let's see if we can tackle that jigsaw puzzle."

When Kate and Danny returned to the living room, the television was off. The adults had gone to the kitchen for coffee, and radio music could be heard in the background. For a few minutes, the kids just worked on the puzzle. Then Uncle Dave came in and stood by the card table.

"They just had a news bulletin on the radio. Oswald didn't survive the surgery. He died from a ruptured aorta."

Scott stared at his dad. "Kate's right; now we'll never know the whole truth."

CHAPTER THIRTEEN

"May the angels, dear Jack, lead you into Paradise."
Cardinal Cushing, November 25, 1963

K ate awakened early on Monday morning and
lay in bed wondering if anyone else was up yet.
Her cousins were both bunking in Danny's room, and
her aunt and uncle were in the guestroom next door.
They had all stayed up late working on the puzzle and
digesting the fact that Lee Harvey Oswald was dead.
Three days ago, she had never heard of the man; now
his name was as familiar as John Wilkes Booth's.

With no confession from the suspected assassin,
the television commentators had speculated endlessly
on whether Oswald had acted alone or was part of a
larger conspiracy. A handful of bystanders, including
Kate's own mother, were still convinced they had heard

shots from the top of the grassy knoll. Yet the only solid evidence collected by the investigators pointed at Oswald and only Oswald. Would they ever know the truth?

And what about Jack Ruby? Why would a nightclub owner in Dallas feel compelled to commit an act for Jackie? It seemed preposterous that Ruby was so devoted to the Kennedys that he wanted to save the first lady the heartache of having to return to Dallas to testify at Oswald's trial, yet that was exactly what Ruby had told the police. He seemed stunned that he had been booked as a murderer rather than heralded as a hero. Was there a possibility that Ruby himself was part of some conspiracy to silence Oswald? These thoughts occupied Kate's thinking.

It wasn't until 8:30 that she heard doors opening and the sound of voices. Kate was already dressed and ready to face one more day immersed in the aftermath of the assassination. Not until tomorrow could she truly try to put these events behind her. Then again, tomorrow had its own bad smell. Tomorrow she had to go back to school and face her friends. For now, however, she had the comfort of family. Tomorrow could wait.

Kate walked into the kitchen where her mother and aunt were busy preparing breakfast. Neither looked like they had slept well. Their drawn faces and red-rimmed eyes gave testimony to the same thoughts that were tormenting Kate. "Need any help?"

"Oh, good morning, Kate. We were just deciding what kind of eggs to fix. What do you think?"

"I vote for scrambled. That should suit everyone." Kate walked to the silverware drawer and counted out knives, forks, and spoons. She noticed that her dad had put the extra leaf in the kitchen table so that all eight of them could squeeze around it.

Uncle Dave walked in with the morning paper. This time the headlines screamed out the jailhouse shooting. A large front-page photo captured an open-mouthed Oswald as he felt the impact of the bullet that had claimed his life. "It says here that when Oswald was first taken to Parkland, they started to roll him into the exact same room where Kennedy died. Fortunately, someone noticed and had him put in another room."

"Wow, that would have really been something, huh?" Kate's mom shook her head. "It would have been ironic if both men had died in the same room just forty-eight hours apart."

"Good morning, everyone." Kate's dad walked into the kitchen with a pleasant smile on his face. Always the optimist, Frank Gallagher could be counted on to cheer the family up as much as possible. "Something smells good."

"Cindy made her famous biscuits. Everything's just about ready, so Kate, why don't you see if the boys are awake."

Kate knocked on the door to Danny's room. "Hey, guys. Breakfast is ready. Rise and shine." She went back to the kitchen and helped pour orange juice for everyone.

Scott came in and sat down just as Danny and Jeff made their first appearance. Everyone laughed at the sight of Jeff's hair sticking straight up. It felt good to laugh, and soon everyone was busy eating and making small talk.

Later, after showers had been taken, the dishes had been cleared and washed, and the beds had been made, the two families gathered once again in front of the television. They were amazed to learn that, since yesterday afternoon, an estimated two hundred and fifty thousand people had stood in line to walk through the capitol's rotunda and pay their final respects to President Kennedy. Many people had braved the cold overnight temperatures in order to file past the draped coffin.

Television reporters explained how Jacqueline Kennedy had personally planned the state funeral using many of the same ideas from the funeral of Abraham Lincoln. One difference, however, was that the body of John Fitzgerald Kennedy would be buried in Arlington

National Cemetery rather than in his family plot in Massachusetts.

"Did you know that both Kennedy and Lincoln had vice presidents named Johnson?" Jeff told them.

"Yeah, but even weirder, Kennedy's secretary was named Mrs. Lincoln and Lincoln's secretary was named Mrs. Kennedy," said Scott. "I read that somewhere."

"I never knew that." Kate turned to her father. "Dad, remember when I showed you that article talking about the twenty-year jinx on the presidency? In the past century, a president has died in office every twenty years."

At noon the televised coverage began by showing the procession from the capitol rotunda to St. Matthews Cathedral. Jacqueline Kennedy had announced that she would walk behind the cortege. Today the first lady was once again wearing a black suit and gloves, but this time she also wore a black gossamer veil and hat. Bobby and Teddy, the only two surviving Kennedy brothers, wore long mourning coats and accompanied the widow. What she did not realize when she made the decision to walk behind the caisson was that the large entourage of special dignitaries who had come for the funeral would choose to join her as well.

Throngs of people lined the streets as the caisson rolled by. Kate and Scott were amazed at the number of foreign dignitaries in attendance. They took turns calling out the names of the kings, queens, generals, and prime ministers they recognized in the crowd. The TV commentator noted that General Charles de Gaulle was present in spite of the fact that he himself had received several death threats for the day. The Secret Service and CIA tried to convince the tall and striking leader of France to forego the funeral rather than endanger his life, but he had refused. He felt it would be disrespectful to the first lady if he were not present. After all, she was part French, and his people had fallen in love with her when she had accompanied Kennedy to Paris six months earlier.

At 12:15, the cortege reached the doors of St. Matthews. As Cardinal Cushing sprinkled holy water on the coffin, the funeral began. Because of his special relationship with the Kennedy family, the cardinal from Boston presided at the service. It would take over an hour for the Latin Mass to be completed.

Feeling restless, Kate got up and looked out the front window. Then she opened the front door, walked out, and sat down on the front steps. She wasn't too surprised when the three boys came out to join her.

"Listen to how quiet it is." The kids looked up and down the normally busy boulevard. Not a car was in sight.

"Wonder how many people are inside watching television?" Jeff asked.

"I bet thousands of people are glued to their sets just like we've been," Danny answered.

"And not just here either. The service is being broadcast all over the world. They've even shut down the Panama Canal."

The cousins continued to talk about things they'd read in the paper or heard on TV. When they were hungry, they went back inside to fix lunch and see if the service was over.

With the Mass concluded, the television camera focused on the Kennedy family as they were ushered outside. Inside, the pallbearers shouldered the coffin and carried it out to the waiting gun carriage. As the family stood in silence, the coffin passed before them. Little John-John gave a crisp salute.

"Look at that," Cindy McDonald marveled. "That child is telling his daddy good-bye." Her voice cracked as large tears ran down her cheeks.

Barbara Gallagher also began to cry as she clutched her sister's hand.

"I read in the paper that John-John is three today. Some birthday," Danny said.

Scott abruptly got up and left the living room.

Kate followed him to the kitchen, where he was getting a soft drink.

"I don't think I can watch much more of this," he said.

"I know; I feel the same way. I don't want to miss anything, but I feel weighed down by it all. I just want things to get back to normal." Kate got herself a Coke and sat down at the table.

"Things will never get back to normal. Nothing will ever be the same again."

"Funny, that's what my mom told us right after it happened."

"Well, she's right. How do we know that Oswald acted alone? What if some guys in the government were involved? One of my friends said he'd even heard rumors that Johnson was involved so he could become president. Isn't that ridiculous?"

Kate thought about it. "I always thought America was too modern and too safe for something like this to happen. Sure, I've read about assassinations in history books and heard of them happening other places, but not here. Never here. At least not since Lincoln."

"What are you guys talking about?" Danny, shadowed by his younger cousin, came in and sat down at the kitchen table.

Jeff opened the refrigerator to find a root beer and then joined the group at the table.

"We're just trying to make sense of everything. Wondering if things will ever be the same," Kate replied.

"I heard Uncle Dave say there will probably be some big investigation even though the Dallas police have said the case is closed."

"Maybe." Scott finished the rest of his drink and stood up. "One thing's for sure; having LBJ as president will not be the same as having the Kennedys in the White House. It was nice having a young president for once."

"I already have a Kennedy scrapbook," Kate said, "and I'm going to save all the newspapers from these past few days. Someday I'll tell my kids how I stood on the grassy knoll." She got up. "Come on; let's go see what's happening now."

The four cousins went back to the living room and watched the procession arrive at Arlington National Cemetery for the burial service. Because John Kennedy had served in the armed forces, he was eligible to be buried there among the 120,000 other veterans who had fought for their country. His final resting place was to be a beautiful hillside with the Lee mansion in the background and a panoramic view of the Lincoln Memorial in the front.

The graveside rites were brief. Fifty jet planes, one for each state, flew overhead followed by the blue and white *Air Force One* flying alone. The band played the national anthem and eyes shimmered with unshed tears as emotions ran high. Cardinal Cushing offered a final prayer that was followed by a twenty-one-gun salute. The military honor guard folded the flag covering the casket. "Taps" was played, and the triangular-folded flag was presented to the widow. Hand in hand, Jacqueline and Bobby Kennedy turned and walked away.

It was finally over.

CHAPTER FOURTEEN

"There are few events in our national life that unite Americans and so touch the hearts of all of us as the passing of a President of the United States."
Chief Justice Warren, November 24, 1963

Once the television coverage concluded, the McDonalds were eager to get on the road. Kate helped them gather their belongings and load the trunk. Barbara Gallagher gave her sister a long hug while the men shook hands and Kate and Danny walked their cousins to the car, reluctant to see them leave. Promising to talk again soon, they all waved as the station wagon backed out and headed off.

Kate saw that her mother's shoulders sagged a little once her sister had left. It had helped to share the sadness and the grief with close relatives. Now, a long empty evening stretched before them.

"I don't know about the rest of you, but I need to get out for a while. Who wants to go over to White Rock Lake and walk around?" Frank Gallagher had a twinkle in his eye. Count on him to recognize the need for a distraction.

"I do, I do!" Danny did a little jump and grabbed his dad's arm in glee.

"What about you, Kate? And Barbara?"

"Okay. I'm ready for a change of scenery." Barbara Gallagher turned to her daughter. "Kate?"

"Sure. But I want to put on my sweatshirt first." Everyone headed in for jackets and sweatshirts before loading into the car.

The lake was located right in town, but it took about twenty minutes to drive there thanks to a noticeable increase in traffic. "Looks like everybody is suddenly getting out; I guess we aren't the only ones who want to shake out the cobwebs," their dad commented as he pulled into the parking lot.

White Rock Lake was the city's reservoir. On one side of the lake were lovely residential homes, but parks and trails surrounded the rest of the lake. It was a favorite destination for locals. On this beautiful fall day, it was the natural place for a walk. Kate noticed several families out and about along with people walking dogs, parents pushing strollers, and a few bikers riding by.

"Wonder how many of these people were here earlier today?" Danny picked up a stick and began picking at the bark.

"I'll bet most of them have been watching the funeral just like we have. But after a while you get cabin fever. It feels good to get outside." Kate gazed up at the sun, took in a deep breath, and let the cool air cleanse away as much of the gray gloom as possible.

The Gallaghers spent about an hour walking around and enjoying the outdoors. No one mentioned the assassination. By the time they drove home, the streets were as jammed as rush hour. It appeared that everyone had decided to try to put the tragedy behind them and get on with their lives.

Kate heard the phone ringing as her mother unlocked the front door. She rushed past her mom and made a quick grab for the phone. "Hello."

"Kate? I've been trying to get ahold of you. Where have you been?"

"Oh, hi, Judy. We went over to White Rock Lake to walk around for a while."

"Did you watch the funeral?"

"Of course. We've done nothing but watch television the past couple of days. My cousins came yesterday, but they left right after the funeral ended."

"I was wondering if I could come over and talk to you." Judy seemed a little awkward, not her usual self.

"Sure. I'm not going anywhere. Come on over." Kate hung up the phone and went to tell her mother that Judy was stopping by.

"Wonder what she wants?" Her mother hung up her jacket and then turned toward the kitchen. Kate followed her.

"She sounded kind of funny. She probably wants to talk about the slumber party." Kate watched her mom take a package of ground meat from the refrigerator and gather the ingredients for meat loaf. "Would you please get out four potatoes to bake?"

Kate washed the potatoes and wrapped them in foil while her mother preheated the oven and continued to mix the meat loaf.

"Remember how I'm supposed to report to my social studies class on our trip to see the president?" she asked her mom. "Do you think Mr. Barrett will still expect me to do it?"

"I don't know. Are you worried about it?"

"Yeah, I don't want to do it. Most of those kids were so critical of the president that I don't want to stand up there and try to describe what we saw to people who don't even care."

"Well, like it or not, you were a key witness to an event in history. You know what it's been like to study the Lincoln assassination. Now the Kennedy assassination will get just as much coverage, maybe even more. You saw history, Kate, and Mr. Barrett will probably want you to share that. For the rest of your life, you're going to hear people ask each other where they were when they learned that JFK had been shot. It's one of those things that people will always remember, and you and Danny will remember it much more than most. In fact, it might be a good idea to write down everything from these past four days while it's still fresh in your memory."

Just then the doorbell rang.

Kate greeted Judy, and the two girls went to Kate's bedroom where they could have some privacy.

"How have you been?" Judy wanted to know.

Kate knew this was her friend's way of trying to find out whether she had gotten over the scene at the slumber party.

"I've been okay. Just sad watching all the TV stuff. Danny and I were both watching when Oswald was shot, so we saw that happen, too."

"I was still at the slumber party. We stayed up half the night so we slept in and didn't eat breakfast until late. But Mr. Gleason came running downstairs to tell us it happened."

"Did anyone even care?"

"Of course they did! Well, maybe not everyone. Linda didn't even know who Oswald was, if you can believe that."

Kate just nodded.

"Kate, I really came over to say how sorry I am."

"Why? You didn't do anything."

"Yeah, that's just it. I didn't do anything. I should have stuck up for you when Gail mouthed off. I should have left like you did. Brenda came back downstairs and told everyone you were going home. She said you were acting stupid and wouldn't listen to reason."

"I'm not surprised. She was pretty mad when I left, but I just couldn't stay after that. It's hard to explain, but being there on the grassy knoll changed me."

"What do you mean?"

"I feel older. I feel sad, like something is gone forever. I know that sounds silly, but it's the truth. I guess that's what people mean when they talk about a loss of innocence. I never believed something this bad could happen until last Friday. A week ago, I would have been worried sick if Brenda had turned against me. But now it doesn't seem very important."

"We're still friends, aren't we?"

"Sure we're friends, Judy. I just need some time to get over this. I never thought for a minute that you were going along with Brenda and some of the others. I know you're not like that."

"Even so, I feel pretty lousy about the whole thing. Watching that funeral today was one of the saddest things I've ever seen. My parents didn't vote for Kennedy, but my mom and I were both crying—especially when that little boy saluted the casket."

"John-John. His nickname is John-John."

"You're going to school tomorrow, aren't you?"

"Yeah, I'll be there. I'm not ready for the science test, but probably I'm not the only one. At least I have the math done, thanks to you."

"Well, I'd better go. It's starting to get dark and I told my mom I wouldn't stay long."

Kate stood up and walked Judy to the front door. "I'll walk you to the corner."

The two girls walked in silence. Kate said good-bye at the stop sign and turned to head back home. Dusk had dropped its smoky cloak, and the air was getting chillier. She inhaled the aroma of wood-burning fireplaces and looked at the golden glow of lights coming from houses up and down the block. On the surface, things looked like they always did, but that didn't fool her for a minute. She knew better.

That night after dinner, Kate went to her room to spend some time alone. She thought about what her mother had said to her earlier. Maybe it would be a good idea to write down her experiences.

She found some paper and spent the rest of the evening recording everything she could remember about Friday and the days that had followed. Occasionally a lump formed in her throat, but she still could not release the tears she wanted to shed. Eventually she ran out of words and put the pages away.

Flexing her cramped fingers, she began getting ready for bed. She was absolutely drained, but the writing had been a good idea. Setting the words to paper had allowed her to put some of the images to rest. Maybe she'd sleep better tonight.

CHAPTER FIFTEEN

*"Ask not what your country can do for you;
ask what you can do for your country."*

John F. Kennedy, January 21, 1961, Inauguration
Address

Kate awoke early after the first sound sleep she'd had in several days. She glanced at the bedside clock and saw that her mother would be up soon. She turned on a lamp and reached for the pages she'd written the night before. She read them through and began to think about what she'd tell her social studies class. She knew that everyone would be interested in what she'd seen, but it seemed too personal to share. She had genuinely admired President Kennedy and was devastated by his death, so how could she give an objective talk about the motorcade?

She couldn't. It was as simple as that. If she stood up in front of the class, it would be impossible to hide her feelings. Just look at what had happened at Brenda's. No, she couldn't do it.

With her decision made, Kate felt better about going back to school.

When she heard her mother knock on her door, Kate called out, "I'm awake, Mom. I'm heading for the shower."

At breakfast, the family fell into its normal weekday routine. As they ate oatmeal, their dad leafed through the morning paper and made comments about several stories. The radio played softly in the background as they talked about after-school plans and the upcoming Thanksgiving holiday. Soon it was time to leave. Kate and Danny kissed their mother good-bye and headed to the car with their father.

"Kate, your mom said you were having misgivings about talking to your social studies class," her dad said as they drove to school.

"Yeah, I'm going to go in early and see if I can find Mr. Barrett. I think he'll understand if I tell him I don't want to do it."

"I'm supposed to talk to my class too," Danny added. "I guess I'll still do it."

"Do whatever you want to; no one will force you," their dad advised.

They rode silently until Mr. Gallagher slowed to a stop in front of the junior high and told Kate to have a good day. She leaned over to kiss him good-bye and then turned to give Danny a quick smile.

"Good luck, Danny."

He nodded as she slammed the door and crossed the street.

Kate had already made her mind up to avoid joining her usual group. Kids were standing outside the building since it wasn't raining. The only ones allowed inside this early were kids with notes or those getting tutored. Kate had a note for her Friday absence, so she headed straight for the door, but she couldn't help but notice that Gail and some of her friends watched her every step. Kate held her head a little higher and didn't let on that she saw them whispering about her.

After Kate collected her excused absence slip from the office, she walked down the hall to the science classrooms. She was relieved to find her science teacher sitting at her desk.

"Mrs. Stryker? I came by to talk to you about the test. I have an excused absence for Friday afternoon. I thought I'd be back and would get my books to take home, but we never got back here. I didn't have my stuff to study for the test."

Mrs. Stryker smiled at her. "Don't worry. I'm postponing the test until tomorrow. I don't think anyone will have studied for it, so it seems pointless to have it today."

"That's great. Thanks." Kate left the lab and turned down the next hallway to see if Mr. Barrett was in his room. Her luck held as she found him writing on the board.

"Mr. Barrett?"

"Oh, hi, Kate. What can I do for you?"

"I know you wanted me to tell the class about going to the president's motorcade, but I don't think I can. I just wanted you to know."

Mr. Barrett turned around and walked over to her. He studied her face and saw the tension in her eyes. He sat on the front edge of his desk. "Did you go?"

"Yeah, we sure did. We were at Dealey Plaza, right there on the grassy knoll. It was awful, Mr. Barrett. My brother and I were standing about twenty yards away when the shooting started. We were even closer for the last shot." Kate felt the panic rising and took a deep breath.

"Is it too hard to talk about?"

"Yes and no. That's just part of it. I mean, I know that I witnessed history. And I wouldn't mind sharing that if I thought the class cared, but I know they don't." She went on to explain what had happened to her on

Saturday at the slumber party and how many of her friends were now talking about her.

"You know, Kate. I have an idea. I'm planning to start the class off with some journal writing and I think it might help bring them around. Let's do this. Why don't you see how it goes and how you feel? I sure don't want to coerce you into talking if you don't feel like it, but describing what you saw might make it a lot more real for everyone. But, you come to class and decide. Whatever you think, I'll support you. Okay?"

"All right. Thanks, Mr. Barrett. I'll see you later." Kate turned and left the room.

◆◆◆◆◆◆◆◆◆

School seemed more subdued than normal, more like a sleepy Monday morning than a couple of days before a national holiday. The teachers pointedly refrained from talking about the assassination and seemed determined to keep business as usual.

Kate kept to herself during the first two periods, but many of her friends were in her third period class with Mr. Barrett. Everyone seemed a little quiet today as they entered the classroom. They all knew it was inevitable that they would discuss the weekend since Mr. Barrett always devoted a large amount of time to current events.

"Class, I want you to take out your response journals and spend the next few minutes reflecting and writing about what I have written on the board." He pulled up a large roller map that had covered the writing prompt. Kate read it silently to herself.

It was reported that after former President Warren Harding heard about the assassination of President McKinley, a neighbor child said to him, "Mr. Harding, I'm sorry your president died." Harding replied, "Son, he was your president, too. He was everybody's president." But the child shook his head and answered, "He wasn't ours. My Mom and Daddy didn't vote for him. He didn't mean anything to us."

After thinking about the words and everything that had happened, Kate picked up her pen and began to journal her response. The scratching of pens, an occasional cough, or the turning of a page were the only sounds that penetrated the silence as her classmates devoted themselves to writing. For ten minutes, no one said anything. Finally, Mr. Barrett told them to take a minute to finish.

Kate concluded her remarks and brought her attention back to her classmates. She looked around the room carefully. A couple of the girls from the slumber party, Brenda especially, avoided eye contact or looked away when Kate glanced their way.

"Who's willing to share what they wrote?" At first no one volunteered, but Mr. Barrett just sat waiting patiently until someone finally said they would start. As one and then two students shared, Kate began to sense a shift in the class. Now there were three or four hands in the air. When called upon, classmates shared some of the same thoughts she had written. Then she saw Brenda raise her hand. Mr. Barrett called on her.

"I don't want to read exactly what I wrote because it's too personal. But I just wanted to say that, at first, I was like that little child. I didn't think Kennedy was my president and I couldn't understand why everyone was making such a big deal out of the assassination. Then I watched the funeral yesterday, and I felt terrible. I watched Jacqueline Kennedy and those two little kids and I felt awful." Brenda paused, swallowed hard, and then continued. "My parents didn't support JFK and I won't sit here and pretend they did. I didn't like everything that Kennedy did; in fact, I didn't like anything he did. But no one should have killed him." Brenda's voice cracked and she began to cry quietly. Mr. Barrett passed her a box of tissues and she dabbed at her eyes. "I guess he really was my president after all." Several other girls had tears in their eyes while most of the boys looked uncomfortable.

"I think Brenda has made a good point." Mr. Barrett went on. "You don't have to have liked President Kennedy to feel bad about the assassination. After all, we're a political country and his politics weren't everyone's politics. But he was *our* president. He was everybody's president, and you should feel outraged that someone shot him. You can feel sad, but mostly you should feel mad. Someone right here in our own city shot and killed our elected leader." Mr. Barrett walked over to the side of the room and leaned against the wall. "You can put your journals away now, class." After a pause, he asked, "Kate, is there anything you'd like to add to our discussion?"

Kate looked into Mr. Barrett's eyes and knew this was her opening. He was allowing her to decide for herself whether she wanted to share her experiences. She looked around at the faces of her classmates, kids she had known most of her life. Gone was the smugness she had expected to find. She glanced at Brenda and saw her give her a little nod. Kate stood up and walked to the front of the classroom.

"Last Friday, I went to see the presidential motorcade with my family. We stood on the grassy knoll." Kate paused to wipe a tear that coursed down her cheek. She saw the intense interest on the faces of her peers and took a deep breath. "My brother and I stood on the grassy knoll about twenty feet from where the president passed."

As Kate described history, the cleansing tears flowed.

REFERENCES

Bishop, Jim. *The Day Kennedy Was Shot*. New York: Funk and Wagnalls, 1968.

Manchester, William. *The Death of a President*. New York: Harper and Row, 1967.

Moore, Jim. *Conspiracy of One*. Fort Worth: The Summit Group, 1990.

Stein, R. Conrad. *The Story of the Assassination of John F. Kennedy*. Canada: Regensteiner Publishing, 1985.

United Press International. *Four Days*. New York: American Heritage Publishing Co., 1964.

AFTERWORD

Just a few days after the tragic events in Dallas, President Lyndon B. Johnson, the thirty-sixth president of the United States, signed Executive Order No. 11130 creating a special commission to investigate the assassination of John Fitzgerald Kennedy on November 22, 1963. Chief Supreme Court Justice Earl Warren was named chairman of the seven-person committee also made up of two senators, two congressmen, and two well-known Americans.

The commission was directed to evaluate all the facts and circumstances surrounding not only the killing of the president but also the subsequent murder of the alleged assassin, Lee Harvey Oswald. The commission was empowered to prescribe its own procedures and to employ such assistance as was deemed necessary.

On December 13, 1963, Congress enacted a joint resolution giving the Warren Commission the power to issue subpoenas requiring the testimony of witnesses and the production of records relating to any matter under its investigation. The commission selected J. Lee Rankin, former solicitor general of the United States, to serve as its general counsel.

Beginning with the day of the assassination, the Federal Bureau of Investigation conducted approximately 25,000 interviews and re-interviews of persons believed to have possible knowledge of the tragedy. In September, 1964, the bureau turned over to the commission approximately 25,400 pages of information. The Secret Service submitted another 4,600 pages of material from the 1,550 interviews they conducted.

In addition to this tremendous amount of data, the commission conducted its own hearings beginning in February of 1964. The commission took the testimony of 552 witnesses. The hearings were closed to the public unless the witness requested that it be open. The commission was concerned that any leakage of these testimonies might lead to premature speculation on what its ultimate findings would be.

Central to the commission's investigation was an amateur home movie shot by Abraham Zapruder, a dress manufacturer, who stood on the grassy knoll and used an 8-millimeter movie camera to capture the motorcade. This twenty-six-second film is the best record of the actual event and has been critical in determining the timing of the shots.

On September 24, 1964, all twenty-six volumes of the Warren Commission Report were delivered to the White House. The report was made available to the public four days later. The initial reaction was one of relief, for the commission found that Lee Harvey Oswald acted alone and there was no conspiracy or link between Jack Ruby and Oswald. The commission concluded its report by making several recommendations for changes in presidential security.

It wasn't long, however, before critics began to question many of the commission's findings. Most controversial was the "magic bullet" theory where one bullet (found in excellent "pristine" condition on a stretcher in the emergency room) was supposed to have been responsible for a combined total of seven wounds on the president and Governor John Connally. Also unexplained was how bystander James Tague came to be wounded by a passing bullet that could not have come from the Book Depository.

Conspiracy theories have abounded in the more than five decades since the death of President Kennedy. More than seventy books, hundreds of articles and interviews, dozens of websites, and one major motion picture have questioned whether the assassination was really the doing of one man and whether that man was even Lee Harvey Oswald. To confound the mystery, the government has sealed many of the records of the assassination until most of the people who were alive at the time are dead.

Another strange fact that has caused speculation on what really happened in Dallas on November 22, 1963, is the fact that eighteen material witnesses died within three years of the assassination. Six died by gunfire, three in car wrecks, five from natural causes, and two were murdered.

The City of Dallas also suffered in the aftermath of the shooting. Public opinion polls indicated that over eighty percent of Americans had indicted "the people of Dallas" for the crime. Joe M. Dealey, grandson of the community builder, was quoted as saying, "We are a tormented town."

It was seven years before the Dallas community erected any kind of memorial to John F. Kennedy. At first, city officials just tried to make the nation forget the assassination had taken place in Dallas. No one seemed to blame Memphis for the murder of Dr. Martin Luther King Jr. or Los Angeles for the slaying of Robert Kennedy in 1968, but JFK's murder continued to be strongly connected in people's minds with Dallas. It was publicity the city did not want.

Finally, on June 24, 1970, the city dedicated a park called John F. Kennedy Memorial Plaza a few blocks from where the shooting occurred. Simple in design, with nothing at the site connected to the shooting, the park seldom attracted tourists seeking comfort or answers to the national tragedy.

Millions of visitors, however, kept returning to Dealey Plaza to see the actual setting of the slaying. Over the years, Dallas residents became accustomed to seeing visitors surveying the intersection of Commerce and Elm while they climbed the grassy knoll and took pictures from numerous angles. Finally, in 1989, twenty-five years after the assassination, a sixth floor exhibit was opened to the public in the Texas Book Depository building. Designers of the exhibit re-created the sixth floor to duplicate the way it looked when Oswald worked there. The rest of the exhibit contains photographs, videos, and documents related to the event. Visitors can view the Zapruder film in its entirety as well as see black and white footage of the news coverage from 1963.

In October of 1993, the Dealey Plaza site was designated a National Historic Landmark. An official dedication ceremony occurred on November 22, 1993, on the thirtieth anniversary of the tragedy. Nellie Connally, wife of Governor Connally, dedicated a bronze landmark plaque that reads: "To future generations of Americans, with the hope that the legacy of John F. Kennedy will inspire them to reach for greatness in their own lives."

Today the Sixth Floor Museum at Dealey Plaza welcomes thousands of visitors annually.

ABOUT THE AUTHOR

Nancy Connors is a retired educator and attorney residing in the Dallas Metroplex with her husband Tom and her cat, Charlie. During her forty years as an educator Dr. Connors found that students gravitate to good stories. In her classroom teaching days she chose teaching novels as a springboard to student research and inquiry while simultaneously introducing students to the love of reading.

Nancy has long been interested in the questions and mystery surrounding the 1963 Kennedy assassination. By capturing the assassination in an eyewitness account based on facts and her own experiences, this story describes the event for those too young to know.

Honored as a Texas State Reading Teacher of the year, Dr. Connors spent her career as a reading consultant, a university adjunct professor, a writer, and a family attorney. She's trained teachers across the country, written professional articles, classroom curriculum, and test passages for grades six through twelve. This is her first novel.

CPSIA information can be obtained
at www.ICGtesting.com
Printed in the USA
LVOW13s1614210518
577956LV00021B/490/P